D0996445

THE DAY OF THE FOX

By the same author

SAMARA
WITHIN THE LABYRINTH
A SINGLE PILGRIM

•

A DRAGON APPARENT
GOLDEN EARTH

The
DAY of the FOX

A NOVEL BY

NORMAN LEWIS

Frazer says that in Celtic times foxes were burned in midsummer fires, being supposed to be under the spell of witchcraft or to be witches who had transformed themselves into animals for the purpose of prosecuting their plots against the welfare of mankind. It is perhaps for this reason that the fox is still considered a beast of ill omen in many parts of modern Europe.

THE REPRINT SOCIETY
LONDON

FIRST PUBLISHED 1955
THIS EDITION PUBLISHED BY THE REPRINT SOCIETY LTD.
BY ARRANGEMENT WITH JONATHAN CAPE LTD. 1957

PRINTED IN GREAT BRITAIN BY RICHARD CLAY AND COMPANY, LTD.
BUNGAY, SUFFOLK

CHAPTER I

IN the morning, when the sea was still white and calm, as if with the concealed heat of molten metal, when among the fishermen the general movement was away from the sea to the land, to wife, to bed, or tavern, the fisherman Sebastian Costa untied his boat and pushed off from the shore.

Costa, a man who contemplated suicide fairly often, fished alone always. For him, since it was already May, the bitter, silent, unruffled months of summer had come. In winter, a man on his own could make some sort of a living clearing out the rock pools, or spearing the big fish by torchlight when, of a calm night, they came in to sleep in shallow water. But summer was hopeless. Summer emptied the coastal waters. You had to get together and plan something like a military campaign to defeat summer. Twelve men, for example, to handle a small sardine boat. Three or four men plus a horse and cart to carry one of the big nets down to the shore. Even the line fishermen who worked in pairs had to keep on the right side of a little clique of specialists who caught the live-bait. It amounted to being clever enough to marry the Plain Jane whose widowed mother owned a big boat. Or failing that, having the luck to be a second cousin of a chap who had inherited a couple of complete sets of tackle. Or even to have been in the prison camp after the war with the fellow who looked after the boats' engines.

Or in the last resort, it was a good thing even to be a friend of a friend of one of these persons. But as it happened, Costa was friendless. He had succeeded in cutting himself off completely.

Circumstances obliged Costa to fish for merous long after the others had given it up as a bad job. Merous were splendid, solitary fish, whose firm flesh was worth more per kilogram than any other in the market. But they were disappearing, and the expert whose father took a fine specimen out of the sea as a matter of daily routine, considered himself lucky to catch a mediocre example in a week's hard fishing. The merous lived in caves in the rocks each in its own chosen hole, growing if given the chance to enormous size, their cunning increasing with the years, until the biggest and oldest became recognized as uncatchable and acquired affectionate nicknames and legendary reputations. There were only about twenty spots along the coast within reach of a rowing-boat which the merous were known to favour, and it was Costa's daily habit to visit these and, with justifiable pessimism, draw up the hook he had baited on the previous occasion, replace the bait, and allow it to sink back into the apparently lifeless depths.

This particular day followed the pattern of the others. A couple of hundred strokes of the creaking, hand-callousing oars, a pause of five minutes for rebaiting, then the long, slow pull again. There was no emotion of any kind in this business. Costa was hardened to disappointment and, in recent years, to joy as well. Even on those rare occasions when he knew from the resistance on his line that there was a fish, a small bitterness would creep in. 'Why couldn't it have been sooner?' he would say to himself. He was a man of thirty-five with arms like tree-trunks, an over-sensitive mouth, a little turned down at the corners by the way life had gone, and an expression as if he had not quite recovered from an unpleasant surprise. An archipelago of big yellow freckles appeared as light patches in the dark red of his face and arms. Costa's reserves of character had been used up in the effort of becoming a superb fisherman, contrary to his inclinations. He hated the sun, which on this day, after thirteen years of the sea, scalded him as remorselessly as it had done when he had first reluctantly carried his tackle down to his father's boat to take up the fisherman's life.

In five hours Costa rowed three miles, took up and rebaited twelve lines, muttered at the sky and the brazen horizon, felt the sun's sting, wiped the sweat continually out of his eyes, and worried about the future. At this moment he was suffering more than ever before from a sense of approaching disaster. He felt the ring of people's hatred closing in to crush him with the indifference and inevitability of a process of nature. Even his childhood sweetheart had at last forsaken him and, although this final calamity had been presented as a matter of economic necessity, he suspected that Elena had thought it kinder to make the break in this way. Nagging fears darkened every moment of the day. He prepared complaints and expressed them, often aloud, to an imaginary third party, a kind of arbiter, seen as a bored old landowner who had lost his taste for life and was therefore fairly neutral in his attitude to the human predicament. 'I never held a grudge against anyone,' Costa would point out. 'Always wanted to do the right thing by all of them, so how can you justify the way they behave? Now take Elena, of all people — she's stopped writing. Really now, that's the last straw. I'd never have believed it of her.'

The arbiter, as usual, had nothing helpful to offer.

Somewhere about midday he hooked a small octopus out of a pool. Catching it by the tentacles as he freed it from the gaff, he lashed out its resistance against a rock, turned its body inside out like a rolled stocking, and extracted with his forefinger a transparent slobber of intestines. He beached the boat and tied it to a stake. Then, trousers rolled over knees, he went back, dropped the octopus into the sea and picked it out again, watching the last of its ink smoke away in the clear water. He climbed the beach, his toes digging into the hot, rasping sand. The octopus roped down from his hand, suckers still faintly mouthing. There were ten thousand gallons of baleful light awash in this bay; a crescent of umbrella pines, stridently green; ravens grunting somewhere in a tin-plate sky.

A shack had been put up at the back of the beach. This had been the labour of a man named after the Saviour, who, having failed at several occupations, had hung on here as long as he could, selling brandy, tins of sardines and stale bread to occasional week-end trippers. When at the end of his tether, he had been accused by the police of some misdemeanour, and had died from the beating received at their hands.

As Costa came up from the water he noticed someone moving about the shack and remembered the report that a new man had taken over the pitch. The shacker seemed to have observed his arrival and now moved out cautiously from the shade towards him, like a spider a little uncertain of what has been taken in its web. Costa was astonished to see that, in spite of his extreme emaciation, he was dressed in jaunty holiday attire, his scraggy, sun-blackened arms protruding from the sleeves of a modish linen jacket. Costa went up to him.

'Do with an octopus?'

The shacker screwed up his face in feigned contempt. Costa knew that shackers would eat anything — moray-eel, seagull, fish-heads. 'All right,' he said. 'Do you want it, or don't you?'

The insect world had come to terms with this man. There were yellow sand ants on his face and hands. The prepared speech crumbled, and meaningless words popped in the air between them: 'Of course, you're well aware ... circumstances permitting ... if an understanding could be reached. . . .'

The splutter of words stopped. He hitched up the fashionable calf-length trousers, then cautiously pushing forward a finger he touched a sucker. The sucker closed over the finger-tip like the mouth of a new-born baby taking the nipple, and saliva wetted the corner of the shacker's lips. 'Hm. Indubitably fresh. What were you asking?'

'Let's have some wine.' The hiss of the sea at his back, greasy, colourless at noon, whispered salt and heat. Costa felt his thirst increase. At the same time he had an acute and disturbing sensation of re-living some fragmentary episode of his past. He had seen this man before. He had said to him those same words, 'Let's have some wine.' And then, as the man turned to take the octopus back to the shack and he saw the limp again, the incredible answer came to him. 'Vasco!' he shouted, 'Vasco!'

The man stopped, turned back slowly. 'Were you addressing me?'

'Vasco,' said Costa, 'You're Vasco, aren't you?' It's either that, or I'm going crackers, he thought.

'Cabrera,' said the man. 'Juan Prudencio Cabrera, at your service.'

Costa followed him, thinking: God knows I've had a bad time. Perhaps this is the way it takes you. 'Vasco, old pal,' he said, 'why try to pull that stuff with me? It isn't as if we weren't together long enough.'

The shacker looked bewildered, but willing to oblige. 'I'm afraid I'm not entirely with you, friend. Should I know you?'

'Should you know me? What a question to ask! Where were you and I in the winter of thirty-eight, for instance?'

The lines in the shacker's face deepened to produce a smile, hardly distinguishable from a grimace of anguish. 'My dear sir, no one wishes more than I do I could help you. The fact is I've had the misfortune to lose my memory.'

'Lost your memory, have you? Well, that's a new one at least!' Costa pushed his face into the shacker's, searching for a tell-tale spark of recognition. But there was none. Neither was there any evasion. The shacker met his gaze with weary tolerance, as in his imagination Costa reformed this face with the flesh that fifteen years had wasted from it. With every second his certainty increased. Now the voice came back, the trick of speech, the small scar over the lip. The scar! . . . that was the answer. 'Look here,' he said, 'I'll prove to you that you're Vasco, whether you know it or not. Why do you limp? I'll tell you why. You got a shell splinter through the thigh. Hardly see where it went in through the front, and a lump of meat as big as my fist missing at the back.' He suddenly grabbed the shacker and found with his fingers the hollow he had described. Shouting with excitement, he flung his arms round the man's neck. A startled ant raced for the shelter of the seaweed hair. The shacker's face twitched violently.

'Vasco, old chap, after all this time! Just imagine it! What on earth have you been up to, you old turkey-cock?' Suddenly Costa's nostrils caught a faint but sickening odour. He drew back.

'I don't know,' said the shacker. 'That is to say I've been a schoolmaster, and so on. But well — you can see how things are. After all, when half your life's practically a blank. The best years.' An eye moistened, and he rubbed his nose with the back of his hand. A gust of hot wind shook the paper flags with which the shack was festooned, as if in celebration of the wedding of a pair of lepers.

'Surely you remember the day we both caught it together, you in the backside, more or less, and me through the throat here?' Costa put up a finger to touch the glossy patch, the size of a small coin, beside his windpipe. Vasco shook his head.

'Neither of us had any time for the Nationals, and when we planned to skedaddle together, they tumbled. Surely you remember that? Now listen here — you can't have forgotten that sergeant of the Ninteenth Navarra who was going to have us court-martialled?'

Vasco's hands shot out desperately, fumbling for words like a fowler groping for the birds in his trap. 'Amazing, absolutely staggering! Court-martialled, you say? Just imagine that! Only a few unconnected incidents. All jumbled up. I was examined by several eminent doctors . . . but the financial angle, you know. But do be seated, please. Perhaps I should do something about the fish?'

'It was terrific,' Costa said. Suddenly he felt a boy again. 'I can hear that sergeant now. "You'll be court-martialled after the show," he said. Between you and me, he was a bastard if ever there was one. You know, he had it in for all us conscripts. Smart enough to know we were only in their army because we hadn't any choice in the matter. "In the meanwhile," he says, "I've got a little surprise for you." I can hear him now. So we find ourselves — just you and me — in a trench fifty yards out in no-man's-land with a duff machine-gun, just before the attack's due. His idea was we would make a run for it, and that would give him the chance to let us have it in the back, with no nonsense about court-martials.'

Vasco said, 'It's not much better than a dream. I mean such incidents as I can recall. Quite unrelated.'

Costa shook his head with wondering sympathy. 'What a terrible thing! It was the biggest joke that ever happened. Of course, we failed to oblige, and decided to stay where we were. When the Reds arrived we hardly had time to give ourselves up when their guns started chucking shells everywhere, and then one dropped in the trench and killed everyone but you and me. So there we were after the counter-attack, still hanging on to our post with dead Reds all round us, a couple of nice easy wounds, and covered in glory. As luck was, the sergeant caught a packet, so there was no one to know any better. A decoration apiece and a couple of stripes was the least they could do. The general himself came down to the base hospital to pin on the medals. Heroes, my boy. That was us. I thought I should never be able to wipe the grin off my face . . . Look here, Vasco, do you mean to say it's all gone? Don't you even remember being a hero?'

The shacker shook his head mournfully. 'Absolutely not, and to tell you the truth it's hard to imagine anyone's miscalculation working out in favour of your obedient servant.' He had moved nearer to Costa along the bench upon which they sat, and now once again Costa caught the faint but sickening odour of death.

'Plums of any kind don't often come my way,' Vasco said. 'What can you expect? But, in strictest confidence, I don't mind telling you that I did have a bit of a windfall a couple of days ago. This.' He took the sleeve of the jacket he was wearing, and fingered it affectionately. 'Perhaps you heard of that sad matter — when was it — last Thursday? — I can't even remember the days of the week now. I'm referring to the boat that capsized. One of those tragedies of the sea.' The shacker rested a hand on Costa's arm and lowered his voice. Beyond the dried-out face a beautiful young lady in an advertisement held out a bottle enticingly, 'The Pause That Refreshes'. 'One of the young fellows involved happened to be washed up. Found him in a pool, somewhat the worse for wear. Understand me, I made it right with the police but, however much of a hero or otherwise one may have been, it's a bit of a temptation to resist when, in any case, they only burn the clothing.'

Vasco got up. 'Well, now to attend to our excellent fish.' He stopped, turning suddenly, and Costa was certain that he had read the disgust in his face, because his expression changed suddenly. 'You know, my memory's quite haywire. What was it now I wanted to ask you? Ah yes, of course. What happened to us after that?'

'After what?'

'We were in hospital – heroes the pair of us weren't we? What happened then?'

There was something about this question that made Costa feel vaguely uneasy. 'Nothing much,' he said. 'There wasn't much more to it.'

'Did we go on seeing much of each other?' Vasco asked. 'What I mean to say is, after they patched us up, were we still together?'

'No,' Costa said, 'not for long. You dropped out of sight. Posted as missing, or something like that.'

'And you,' said Vasco, testing once again the now unresponsive octopus suckers with his finger tips, 'did it take you long to get away?'

'To get away?' Costa was certain that there was malice in his face.

'From the Nationals. That was the plan wasn't it? To make a break for it as soon as we got the chance? Correct me if I'm all mixed up again. I'm going by what you said.'

'I don't know about you,' Costa said. 'Perhaps you did, and perhaps you didn't. But as far as I was concerned, I never got the chance.' He was suddenly irritated with this questioning.

'Oh well, why worry anyway?' said the shacker. 'You were a hero where you were, in any case, and that's not to be sneered at.'

He went off into the shack, leaving Costa wondering: now can that bastard be laughing at me after all? And then, with panic suddenly twisting in his stomach, he thought: this is the way I'm going to finish up, too, if I don't look out.

CHAPTER 2

A NEW edge to his despair, sharpened by his encounter with Vasco, drove him to force more than a day's work into the hours of daylight. Instead of following his normal routine and making for home, Costa decided to row another mile to a bay which was called 'Moors in Hell' because of the tormented rock formations encircling it. Here a cliff had decayed and tumbled into the water, littering the sea's bed with great boulders riddled with caverns and passages offering a perfect refuge for fish. There were a score of acres of this underwater labyrinth to be surveyed, and Costa's tiny window upon the secrets of the sea consisted of a viewing box with a glass bottom a foot square. He set out slowly, disconsolately, hopelessly, to quarter the site, manœuvring into position with the oars, then leaning out over the boat's side to peer through his small peephole into the sea's vast glassy opacity.

Below, revealed piecemeal, square by square, were great, stacked up menhirs, gore-splashed as if from many sacrifices, marked with secret signs, limpet-riveted, studded all over with the alert, tenacious things of the sea. Costa felt mocked by this gaudy, unsubstantial treasure, nothing of which was worth a price; these flowers and corals which would wither, fade and stink if snatched from their setting. Nameless, uncatchable fish darted like dragon-flies from dim recesses, hovered over carmine-splashed rock surfaces, and hid themselves in lavender traceries of weed. The whole bag of tricks, he thought, not worth a peseta. He was sad at the thought that none of this beauty could be made to serve any decent commercial purpose. None of it eatable, he thought. None of it any good for anything. Just imagine that!

'It can't go on much longer like this,' he said out loud. 'I'm at the end of my tether. It's hopeless. Next thing, I'll be selling the boat and going round the farms asking if they want anyone to hoe the beans. Or putting up a shack. Don't forget that. A shack. My God!'

And then, he thought — for the thousandth time — why not clear off . . . go to Cadaques or somewhere? Chance my luck on the sardine boats. The question is, would it get round? How long would it be before someone who knows me — the public messenger for instance — gets to hear about it and pulls a long face in one of the bars? 'Costa — old Costa. Yes, well — let's see now. I hardly know what to say. Difficult to put these things into words — in any case, it's not up to me. Not exactly the kind of thing you like to commit yourself about — if you know what I mean.' And that would be all that was necessary. In these times when people had learned never to come right out with what they meant, no one knew better than these fishermen how to take a hint. In Costa's mind the whole thing had already happened; the smiling, cautious betrayal by the public messenger, his condemnation once again without trial.

At about five in the afternoon, when the light was already weakening and a brown murk of shadows rising slowly from the sea's bed engulfed the bases of the underseas rocks, Costa saw the fish. It was hanging there as if encased in ice, huge and motionless and unbelievable, standing—as merous always seemed to when their curiosity was attracted by something on the surface—on its tail. From this angle he saw only the fish's head pointed directly at him, the pectoral fins extended ruff-like on each side of the head, fanning the water with a slow rhythm. Even Costa, through his encrusted sourness, was thrilled by its beauty and its ugliness; the drooping lower lip of the great depressed mouth, like that of an embittered old man; the eyes goggling with curiosity; the colours living and miraculous, never seen by a landsman, never captured by an artist, purples and violets generated in the body of the fish itself, constantly changing, blushing and paling, instantly extinguished by death.

As the boat drifted over it across the shimmering skin that roofed its world, the merou pivoted, eyes drawn to the boat's shadow, showing only a flickering movement of bone-strutted fins. Suddenly Costa knew that only by killing could he come near to the possession of this beauty. The sale of the carcase of this fish would be a meaningless anticlimax, as trivial a pleasure as the eating of its flesh by those who bought the carcase. Only he, the killer, would know the true pleasure of this fish, linked in some mysterious way to its beauty by the tremendous act of putting it to death.

Now, realizing that the boat's drift was carrying him away, he became alarmed, because it was essential to frighten the merou into betraying itself by retreating to its hole. He splashed frenziedly with his free hand, and in a moment the fish's curiosity gave place to suspicion and its head sank, giving Sebastian a glimpse of its true proportions: the enormous barrel chest, the short body tapering quickly to the small spade-shaped tail. A hundred pounds, he thought. As the fish heeled over, moving with the slow deliberation of a submarine, it displayed the tarnished gold of flanks and belly, and then, sinking and turning, it became inky, bloodily dark against the rocks, colour deepened by the change of perspective, as with hardly a movement of fins or tail it glided with the smoothness of a ship entering harbour into the mouth of its cave.

The air held tightly in Costa's lungs went free. Now he was as sure of himself as if the cave's opening had been the entrance to a trap. He noted the cave's position in relation to the surrounding rocks, amazed that so big a fish should have taken refuge in the shallow water. Then settling down in the boat he began the leisurely preparation of the tackle, the elaborate ceremonial with freshly washed hands, new hook and line, that were the fisherman's tribute to such an opponent.

Costa knew that he was going to hook this fish. He would hook it because it would always be in the same cave awaiting him, and Costa would come day after day to dangle choice bait in the cave's mouth, and one day, perhaps the next, or perhaps in a week's time — but not longer than a week — the merou would come out and swallow the bait. It was then that the real struggle would begin, the struggle to drag up the merou — which in the water had a desperate, stubborn strength more like that of a mule than a fish — from the depths of its private labyrinth. The sea was full of tough old merous with great hooks rotting away in their gullets, or half-digested in their maws, who had come out victors in such struggles.

He finished his preparations, dropped the baited hook over the side, and watched the mackerel, stiff-curved and shining, sink away, its silver quickly water-slaked, as he manœuvred it by delicate shiftings of the boat's position down through the currents to come to rest at the mouth of the cave. Then the rock round which the end of the line was bound went in with a splash, trailing after it its cork buoy. Costa cooled off with a quick dip in the sea and, taking up the oars again, headed for home. Suddenly, for the first time for many weeks, he felt his blood tingle faintly with optimism. He rowed strongly, helped by the tide and a following breeze. A fine, white ship went by drawn smoothly across the horizon. Landwards the cliffs were gay with furze and pines.

As he came into the haven, he saw the foreigners, coloured Japanese figures, dotted about the beach, motionless under their parasols, and heard the released schoolchildren who were playing a ring game and singing: 'And all the pretty little girls they drowned in the sea. Stephen! Stephen! The devil's passing by.'

Costa's boat's keel slashed the shingle. He jumped ashore and tied up. A few of the men were busy getting their gear ready to go out at night. Costa called out a greeting to the nearest of them and one of the group raised his hand.

CHAPTER 3

MARTA, Costa's old mother, was a small, black, hesitant silhouette in the wings of that morning's brilliant stage. She began her cautious descent into the heart of the village, two questions uppermost in her mind — food and fuel.

The morning air rang with jubilant sounds. A forgotten sliver of moon hung in the sky, encircled by screaming swifts. A young man in the church tower was bombarding heaven with explosive rockets to remind that day's saint of the martyrdoms of this world. Servant girls, a little crazed with brief freedom, ran through the streets on their early errands, uttering cries which were pierced through in space by the peacock-screech of the knife-grinder's machine. Marta was delayed for a moment outside the grocer's shop while the horse which pulled the barrel-organ, being released from the shafts, rolled over three times and righted itself with a great clicking of heels. Then the old woman went into the shop. She was a little nervous.

The grocer's establishment was run by the Señorita Rosa, a once-beautiful girl who still wore a little disconsolate youth, like a trivial, poignant flower, fading in the bosom. The shopkeepers of Torre del Mar had almost evolved into a species different from the rest of the population. Whereas the fisherfolk were lean people who might occasionally fatten out a little at the season of the abundant autumnal catches, thereafter returning to their basic proportions, the shopkeepers went on acquiring throughout life a progressive and permanent covering of flesh. But the main difference between these two groups was psychological and lay in their attitude towards money. The fishermen liked to discuss their gains openly and would stop each other in the street merely to announce how much, to the peseta, their latest catches had fetched at auction. They lived on credit through the winter and, whenever a windfall came their way, they would rush off to squander it on impractical furniture for inclusion in a daughter's or sister's dowry. 'Take a look at that, old son. A week's fishing there. No more and no less. A record if ever there was one. And don't go running away with the idea that that's wood either. Plastic all through, every centimetre of it.' 'But what's the big idea of the cocktail cabinet, if neither of them drinks?' 'Oh that? — well never mind. Even if they don't, their kids may. Got to allow for progress, after all.' Shopkeepers weren't like this. Money had reached a higher status in their lives. On the rare occasions when they mentioned it at all, they were inclined to refer to it in such abstract terms as 'expense', and they would never have dreamed of allowing the details of what they made to become public property.

When Marta came in, the Señorita Rosa looked up and past her into space where a private revelation in the form of a series of luminous figures had appeared.

'A small bag of charcoal,' Marta said. 'Not exactly a shipping order this time.' She was hoping to carry off the occasion by the assumption of a casual tone.

Señorita Rosa consulted her figures. Two and three makes five, and eight more thirteen. Less four paid for on the last time but one. That leaves us with nine. Wait a moment while I verify that with the ledger. Nine it is. 'Do you think you could favour us with a trifle on account, Señora? I'm sure you appreciate the difficulty in allowing indefinite credit.'

Sighing, Marta felt in her pocket for two pesetas, picked up the bag and went out. That was the fuel situation settled, at least. She was afraid the matter of the food would prove more difficult to arrange.

A little of the morning's gay infection touched the old lady as she continued her calculated journey, moving from shade to shade down the village street. A faint seasonal excitation prickled in her blood at the spectacle of the foreigners in their outlandish finery, whose numbers were increasing with every day. Summer was announced, too, by the banners of strange clothing streaming from the rooftops of the newly opened villas of the rich Spanish visitors, and each green telephone insulator had become a burning emerald. She stopped by the fountain to rest, and also to watch the antics of a group of strolling players who had set up their tent on the beach. The actors were far more real on the stage than off. A hard sun had burned away all the mystery and the magic, leaving a few crack-jointed carnival figures, slatterns and effeminates, who quarrelled in whining voices. 'It's no use, I tell you. Too late, absolutely a washout. Listen, darling, why don't you do me a good turn and go to hell?'

Marta shook her head wonderingly and moved on. A strange, high-framed motor cycle puttered to a standstill alongside her, its rider an elderly man so straight, so thin and so stiff-looking that one expected to hear a cicada-like creaking when he moved his limbs. The elderly man raised a black hat, attached by a length of elastic to the lapel of his cotton jacket. 'A very good morning, Madame. Might I trouble you to inquire whether your son has any fish to offer?' Don Federico Vilanova was accustomed to address her with the greatest of ceremony.

'He's out now,' Marta told him. 'I don't expect him back for an hour or two. If he catches anything I'll send him up . . . And, by the way, sir, we decided to take your advice and let the spare room.'

'I'm glad to hear it,' Don Federico said. 'Try for an Englishman. Cuckolds all of them, but never mind, they've great dignity in money matters, and are easy to feed. They adore snails.'

Don Federico raised his hat again and, paddling his machine into action, became almost immediately part of that pleasantly diffused pattern into which the world at twenty paces had been transformed.

Food now, she thought. If only I could give him a taste of meat for once, for a change, poor boy. She had reached the doorway of Señorita Antonia's shop and now, groping among the bead curtains, she parted them and went in. The beads clashed behind her, hurling pellets of sunlight and shadow at the Señorita who presided at a counter raised like an altar above the level of the shop, and upon three black-clad customers who crouched below, as if recipients of her ministrations.

The señorita had never found a lover able to throw into the marriage stakes anything capable of counter-balancing the formidable weight of her butcher's shop. She was a stout, smiling girl with flushed cheeks, enormous bosom and varicose veins. Behind her, in final proof of summer's domination — since no meat came to Torre del Mar in the winter months — an immense ox-carcase was suspended from the ceiling. As the fishermen could never afford to buy beef except to give to sick children on doctor's orders, this was intended solely for the consumption of visitors, although the local population would benefit from the availability of such offal as the hotel did not require.

Señorita Antonia, cleaver in hand and swaying a little from weakness in the legs, beamed down while Marta's eyes took in the strange ivory, cinnamon and carmine magnificence of the carcase.

'And what can I do for you, Señora Marta?'

'Well, I was thinking perhaps a little offal.'

'Only what you see there, I'm afraid.' The señorita waved her cleaver at a row of plates ranged along the counter and seemed to blush a little deeper. By stretching herself painfully, Marta saw that these contained the heads and feet of ducks and chickens, little mounds of congealed blood, heaps of miniature organs unidentifiable with gore, and coils of chickens' intestines.

'Meat's too heavy for the stomach. That's my contention,' said one of the three other customers with a disapproving glance at the carcase. At Marta's entry these three old crones seemed to have moved closer together.

'Not even the lights?' suggested Marta.

The señorita shook her head. 'All taken up by the hotel, I'm afraid. Besides, you see, we've got our regulars to think about . . . Take some nice giblets, dear. You can't go wrong with soup.'

'And after all, you've always got the fish your son catches to fall back on,' one of the customers said. The three old women were huddled close, as if reading from the same psalter, united in the sharp joy of malice.

'I hear that things aren't going too well with the fishing these days,' the crone in the centre said.

Marta gave her a sharp glance. 'If there's no fish about, you can't be expected to catch it, can you?'

The Señorita Antonia neatly trimmed off two ducks bills with her cleaver and joined in the conversation. 'Poor boy, he seems to have been out of luck altogether lately. Wasn't it sad about Elena? I expect he was badly cut up.'

Marta seized her opening. 'We most of us have our matrimonial disappointments at one time or another.'

The señorita's smile slipped and straightened itself. She eased the position of her massive bosom among the prime cuts on the counter. 'Well I for one couldn't understand her mother. Letting her go off alone like that!' Her remarks were not addressed to Marta.

'And to Barcelona,' said one of the customers, as if uttering a liturgical response.

'. . . of all places.'

'Still, what can you expect?'

'. . . the circumstances being what they were.'

Marta's thoughts were absent, occupied with the food problem. She had recovered from her disappointment over the offal and was resigned to taking what there was. But was it to be heads and feet, giblets or intestines? Fortunately a half-peseta's worth of onions and tomatoes would so camouflage the choice in the cooking that without taking the lid off the pot it would be impossible to guess from what origins the final relish had been extracted.

The beads clashed again, and the señorita roused herself to deal with another order. 'A plate of giblets, dear? That's right, two pesetas. They're like rubies this morning.' The three old women completed their purchases and went out, and the newcomer turned to Marta.

'I hear you're letting a room, dear.'

Marta started slightly. 'A room? Yes, that's right enough. That's to say we haven't gone any further than thinking about it up to the present.' She was still torn with doubt. For a treat like this she wanted to spend her money to the full effect. If only there had been no choice! Her hand moved uncertainly in the direction of one of the saucers. In the last few minutes their number had halved. Two more shoppers came in. A voice said in her ear: 'But not to a foreigner, surely? That's what they're saying.'

Marta's eye was distracted from the counter for a fatal moment. 'And supposing we do; what's the objection?'

'Objection? Did you hear, for instance, what happened to Carmen? They took down the picture of Our Lord crucified.'

'The women bring men into their rooms.'

'Waiters at the hotel, charcoal-burners even.'

'Go about the house naked.'

' — All got the bad sickness.'

'Might as well throw the mattress away after they've done with it.'

Too late Marta was reminded: it's going to be fish again if I don't look out. She pushed her way to the front again, only to see the last saucer snatched from under her nose. The señorita's peony face beamed down at her. 'Were you wanting something, dear? Why didn't you tell me, and I'd have put it aside?'

Marta went down to the beach. There was nothing for it now. They would eat fish again that day, and on the next morning she would rise earlier than ever, so that at least, come what might, they would be sure of some soup. The thought of chicken soup, about which she had felt so unenthusiastic, made her mouth water now it was out of reach. Tomorrow, she promised herself, they would have soup with potatoes.

A few of the last boats to return were tied up at the water's edge and the men were sorting out their catches for auction. Marketable fish fell into two main categories, 'white' and 'blue'. White fish, such as the mullet, were the choicest the sea had to offer. Apart from its delicate flavour, there was something about this fish which touched the imagination, with the brilliant cherry-red stains welling up through the flesh under the scales as it lay dying in the boat. These the men graded and boxed with affectionate care. 'Blue' fish, which included the mackerel and gold-line, were heaped into baskets and sold without further ceremony. Arañas, technically white, but despised for their insipid flavour and poisonous dorsal fin, were left in the bottom of the boats. Rays and dogfish, considered quite inedible, the men threw back in the water, which was silvered in the shallows round the boats with their diluted reflections.

When Marta reached the boats, there were several

other old women dawdling about. They were all widows, like herself, and all had come to collect what was known as the widows' pension. Most of them were a little diffident in doing this, and while keeping close to the boats they pretended to be bathing their feet, or inspecting nets that had been stretched out there to dry. As soon as the fishermen had finished sorting out their catches they would go away, carrying the boxes and baskets over to the fish market, and the old women would be at liberty to come up and collect whatever was unsaleable, such as the arañas, which had been left for them in the boats. So at the moment of Marta's arrival, with the men in the last stages of their task, the poor widows were slowly drawing nearer and nearer to the boats, where an unknown quantity of treasure awaited them.

It was only in recent weeks that Marta had been able to bring herself to fall in with this custom, and she still felt awkward and ashamed. She was clinging hard to her dignity. She wanted to be last on the scene and to take whatever was left with an inconsequential air. Yet, in doing so, she realized only too well that she risked going empty-handed. She was wavering in the background, undecided, badly placed strategically for the final rush, when she saw one of the fishermen leave his boat and come towards her carrying a box. Too late she recognized him as Celestino, one of the older men, who as a boy had fished with her husband. She was ashamed to be seen there by him, but too slow and too weak to avoid the encounter. She stood there feeling the feebleness of her years as never before, her feet imprisoned in the soft suction of the sand.

Celestino came up to her, stopped and put down the box. Marta glanced down at the tight rows of mullet splashed all over with the brilliant wine of their death-struggles. 'Help yourself, mother,' Celestino said, smiling, 'go on, take a couple of handfuls.'

Marta felt herself flush and was grateful that the tight-scored wrinkles of her face would protect her from the exposure of her shame. The idea of it! It's as if he thought we were on our uppers. She shook her head. 'We've enough of our own. Thank you all the same.'

Celestino picked up the box and walked away without a word. She turned to look after him, furious. To think of that, when my husband taught him all he knows! But now another urgent problem had presented itself, because all the fishermen were leaving the boats, the old women were already closing in, and she could not move from the spot while Celestino was still in sight. Marta waited there stubbornly, watching the man's black shape lose its outlines as the white blotting paper that walled in her world drank it up. Even then she waited, calculating with passionate cunning: although I can't see him, he'll still be able to see me with those young eyes of his.

When she got to the boat there were two small arañas left. She picked them up and put them in her apron. She was thankful.

CHAPTER 4

THE house they lived in had been the labour of a builder whose sub-conscious mind held respectful memories of the cave. So there were no straight lines and all the edges were smoothed away and blunted; the rooms had a comforting concavity and there was no way of deciding where walls became ceilings and rooms passages. It was also evident that the few narrow windows had been pierced as an afterthought and with reluctance. A few sounds from the outside world dropped like figs over the high courtyard walls into a silence only disturbed by discreet internal echoes.

Marta was busy over a charcoal stove in a corner of the courtyard and Costa, sitting nearby on a packing-case, had been trying to bring himself to tackle the old woman on a certain important subject. Once or twice he had taken a preliminary breath and then, his words checked on the verge of utterance, an uneasy silence had developed.

The old woman took the two small arañas, sliced the poisonous dorsal fins out of their backs, cleaned them in a few rapid movements, and dropped them into a pot of boiling water. The sourish, insipid, hunger-stifling smell of the cooking reached him immediately. A lank, cheetah-shaped cat, stretched out on the courtyard wall, woke up and yowled. Costa was a little nauseated. Arañas were only eaten by the fishermen, and what they could not eat themselves they threw back in the sea. There was a premonition of decay in the flesh of this fish, even if eaten within ten minutes of being taken from the net. To-morrow, he thought, he might catch a merou, but they would still eat araña. The merou would sell for the highest price of any fish in the market. A fisherman would have thought it sacrilegious to eat such a fish, and many of them had never tasted its flesh.

'Just settle yourself,' his mother said. 'It'll be ready in a few minutes.' She threw a few herbs into the pot.

'I don't feel particularly hungry,' he said. He knew he wouldn't be able to swallow a mouthful until he had got what he wanted to say off his chest.

He drew breath again. 'Have you ever given any thought to the idea of leaving this place?' His voice had gone unnaturally flat.

The old woman straightened herself to look at him.

'It's about time we looked facts in the face,' he went on hurriedly. 'For example, this place is fished out. I'd make more money sitting out on the beach mending nets with the old crocks. Well, that's the thing in a nutshell, as far as I'm concerned.'

He waited, a little nervous again now that he had had his say, but she was still silent. She was seventy-five years old, and for the last twenty of them she had been shrinking, till now she seemed not much larger than a doll, dressed in changeless, rustling, crow-like black. The years had cancelled out her features with a thousand criss-cross strokes.

'The fact is,' he said, his words coming in a sudden gush, 'I've been going over the possibility of moving to Cadaques or to the Puerto, for the sardine fishing. They're short-handed on the boats. So I've heard.'

'What's to stop you, my boy?'

'Well,' he said, 'naturally you'd have to come along, too. I mean the idea is that we should both go along, and get shot of this place.'

'Sell it, you mean?' she said.

'I suppose that's more or less it. We'd want the money.'

'Sell it to strangers?'

He shrugged his shoulders and pulled down the corners of his mouth. 'You don't get fat on sentiment. If you want to know my opinion, a house is somewhere to sleep, a convenience. You don't want to tie it round your neck.'

A convenience, she thought. For him it was no more than that. But for her it was a temple of the Past, of which she had become an unconscious devotee. She was bound to her home, to this place, not by happy memories, of which she had few, but by a kind of grim understanding reached with the memory of all the tragedies she had undergone there: two revolutions with their church-burnings and the bitter reprisals that had followed; a great epidemic and a great storm, which had kept the village in mourning through the early 'twenties; three sons killed in the civil war, followed by her husband's death, worn-out; the Italian air-raid; her remaining son's misfortunes. These were the true high-lights of her existence. Tears bound her to her house, and to Torre del Mar; every sorrow conquered had infused that ageing body with a little inner strength. Here she lived on in the clean, white, cavernous house which her husband's death had filled with sacred objects — unmoved by present disasters, resigned, fragile, indomitable.

'So you've got your tail between your legs? I must admit I thought you more of a man.'

He could see nothing of her expression, because everything but rare extremes of sorrow and joy was absorbed in the deep screen of wrinkles covering her old face, but there were pity and contempt in the aged voice.

'What else is there for it?'

'You've done nothing except make an idiot of yourself. Stand up to them, my boy. Let them see you've nothing on your conscience. Running away won't do you any good. Put on a bold front and see if they don't come round in the end.'

'How are we going to eat?'

'We've always managed,' she said. 'If the worst comes to the worst, I've never heard of a shortage of acorns.'

And this was her regular argument. Stand up to it! Hold on! Pull in your belt! And in the end everything would work out all right.

But would it? Did she ever realize the deep, confident strength of local antagonism?

He went over in his mind the whole sequence of events. The way things had gone in the first weeks when he had got back to the village, wearing the uniform which he had burned; first the jacket, then the trousers, as soon as he could get hold of civilian clothing. He recalled the slow development of what seemed like a campaign planned by a master intelligence; only, as he knew, it had been quite spontaneous.

First, the sinister refusals to accept anything from him.

They could show no open hostility to anyone who had been on the winning side — the police knew how to deal with that kind of thing — but they were not obliged to put themselves under obligation to him.

'Any time you want the boat, Paco. It's yours for the taking. You know where to find it.'

'Thanks, man. Thanks.' (A smile — always a smile.) He should have realized then that they had sentenced him. That was the moment when he should have understood that sentence had been passed: when the poorest of the fishermen asked nothing from him; when the widows, who were entitled by custom to do so, never took a handful of small fish from his catch; when the beggar never approached him with open hand.

And always the deadly politeness. People never blasphemed in his presence, any more than they did when the priest was about; because a blasphemy shared implied an understanding; men were drawn together under the cloak of the same mild sin.

And then, immediately, all the sardine boats had full crews. Not even a vacancy on a half-share basis to look after the engine or the lights. Even the young ones who had grown up since the war and hadn't any idea what it was all about wouldn't have him in a boat. He was somehow or other unlucky. They wouldn't take the risk of his bringing them bad catches.

'Good day, Sebastian. Blowing up from the west — eh?' No staring, no nudging, no sly remarks. Always very polite.

And then had dawned the terrible day of Elena's departure.

The women of Torre del Mar were prepared to wait ten years for the men of their choice, while the slow, ant-like, laborious accumulation of savings went on, coin by coin, until the day came when the indispensable suite of new furniture could be purchased with which to furnish decently a single matrimonial chamber.

This period had elapsed since Costa had come to an arrangement with Elena, then sixteen. Elena was like a Master's rough sketch for the painting of a very beautiful woman in which some of the less important details had been filled in by a pupil of promise, but to which when it came to the drawing of those sad, enormous eyes, the Master himself had returned to dedicate to them all his love, his skill, and the arrogant confidence of his style. She was thin, tender-hearted and staunch, and Costa, who had come to accept her attachment with dangerous complaisance, was to receive one day in February of that year a terrible shock.

Public meetings between lovers had to be respectably disguised by little acts of horseplay. On this particular occasion Elena was washing clothes at the river bank with the other girls when Costa came strolling by and splashed her by throwing in a large stone. Elena immediately scrambled to her feet and followed him in mock wrath, wiping her hands on her dress. 'I want to see you tonight. Usual time and place.'

The usual place was the cemetery. Here the urgent crises that arise between lovers were settled, and those who were of the opinion that there was nothing to be gained by waiting made love in the darkness, among the tombs. After nightfall there was no recognition between those who passed each other on the cemetery road, the men with their hats pulled down and the women holding handkerchiefs over their faces. All were known to be engaged on the same errand.

'I wanted to write to you,' she said, 'but I didn't know how to put it. I've been feeling terrible. After all, I know it's not your fault, but I've got the old people to think about.'

'Half a minute, I'm afraid I haven't caught on.' Costa found himself short of breath. Ever since the morning his instinct had been warning him to prepare himself.

'My father won't live for ever,' she said. 'You know what they said about his chest. Ask yourself, what's going to happen to my mother. Where will we all be?'

'We'll look after her. She can live with us.'

Elena laughed drily, then put a sympathetic hand on his arm. 'Sebastian, we've never talked about money, have we? In all these years, I've never brought it up once. But don't think I don't know what your position is. Last week the doctor told my father he wasn't to go out fishing any more. How are we going to carry on? I'm speaking for myself as well as my mother. Can you tell me that?'

There was no reasonable answer. Costa produced a few phrases of fumbling reassurance, which sounded meaningless even to him. Elena was crying quietly.

'I must do something. It can't be put off any longer.'

'What *can* you do?' he asked. 'I wouldn't be happy thinking of you working in the hotel.'

'The hotel — don't worry. I've already tried that and there's not a chance. Look here,' she said, 'I may as well tell you now as put it off. I'm sorry, but I'm going to work in Barcelona.'

'You can't possibly,' he said. 'Barcelona, why it's impossible. You go to Barcelona? I'd never agree to it. Just imagine it! Barcelona of all places you could think of.'

'It's all fixed up. With a respectable family. It'll be all right, except we won't be able to see each other very often. Don't be angry,' she said. 'I can't bear you to be angry. I was at my wits' end. I mean, something had to be done.'

'I suppose if the truth's known you found it a bit quiet for your liking here,' he said in a bitter voice. 'They tell me that Barcelona's a very fine place to live in. You'll see plenty of the cinema.' He wanted above all to hurt her now, although of all humanity — his mother apart — only this woman had stood with him, being, as a woman, at the bottom untouched by any causes save those having to do with love, and seeing as only a woman can through the masks that fortune forces over a man's face.

But she had awaited and could allow for this reaction.

'If only you would see it,' she said, 'there's a way out for both of us. Only one way. We could go away together. In Barcelona nobody would know. I could find work in an hotel and you could get a factory job. Why should we worry about having our own furniture? We could get married and live in rooms like they all do in Barcelona. What's to stop your mother coming with us?'

But next day, his mother had shaken her head.

'Far be it from me to stand in your light, my boy. But don't bother about me. There are some things you can do, and some you can't. Not at my time of life, at least.'

This was the answer he had expected.

Next day he carried the tin box containing Elena's possessions down to the little square from which the bus left at midday for Barcelona. He presented her with a Japanese fan and some lavender water, and they said goodbye and shook hands twice when the bus seemed about to start, standing afterwards tongue-tied and embarrassed, only occasionally meeting each other's eyes and exchanging the stiff smiles of those who are dying the small death of parting.

Several neighbours had put in an appearance. 'Well, so-long, Elena. Good trip — eh? Look after yourself, and don't do anything I wouldn't do. You know the kind of place Barcelona is — ha, ha!'

'Just as if he could expect her to . . .' he overheard one of them say.

CHAPTER 5

THE fisherman's fraternity of Torre del Mar met, when there was any business on hand, in a back room of the Twentieth Century Café. Although this body was supposed to concern itself chiefly with such activities as the organization of the annual pilgrimage to the shrine of St. Benedict, its meetings were held *in camera*, even the glum-faced, dried-up old waiter being obliged to tap at the door and wait patiently to be let in. The toil-twisted, unimposing men, bearing between them the names of all the Apostles, who sat here uncomfortably in their stiff, holiday clothes, were the village's shadow parliament and its moral authority. In brief, word-fumbling speeches, they decided the real issues in the life of the community, leaving the mayor and his officials to busy themselves collecting the rates and filling in the holes in the roads.

The fraternity's president, Francisco, was the only man of noteworthy appearance in this assemblage. Francisco maintained an almost dictatorial authority through the possession of certain qualities much admired in a self-denying, puritanical community. Among a people who boasted of the sparseness and the simplicity of their pleasures, the austere and abstemious Francisco was a natural leader. Francisco worked harder, ate less, did not drink, gave more to the charities which the fraternity organized, had spent longer in a prison camp at the war's end. He maintained a large family in unostentatious sufficiency, and his cold, somewhat saturnine good looks had set a-flutter the fanciful heart of more than one northern lady of those who visited Torre del Mar in summer.

This present meeting had been called ostensibly to discuss the raising of funds to enable a villager to undergo an expensive operation in Barcelona. The necessary measures had been agreed in a few nods and monosyllables, and then Francisco said: 'This strikes me as as good a moment as any to advise all present of a step I propose taking next week.'

There were one or two grunts of encouragement.

'I'm thinking of offering Costa a job on my boat. Any objections? No time like the present, if anybody's got anything on his mind.' Francisco threw a severe glance at the semicircle of silent men.

'Well then, I can take it that nobody has any objection. Were you going to say anything, Simón? . . . Sorry if I interrupted.'

Simón, his racked ecstatic's face haloed by a pitted mirror, moistened his lips and said: 'It's your boat, not mine.'

'And you work on it — which makes the matter of special interest to you. Costa'll get a twelfth share now Pedro's dropping out.'

'You're the boss,' Simón said.

'There's a little more to it than that. When Costa joins, every man jack in the boat will shake hands with him.'

'Should we bring a little present of some kind along with us, while we're about it?' Simón asked. 'Half a dozen eggs, or something like that?'

Francisco frowned. 'I just want to make it clear at the start that I'm not prepared to have any bad blood in my crew. We'll all pull together without rancour.'

A man who was being slowly garrotted by his shirt collar said: 'It's your privilege to do what you like with your own property, Francisco. Why shouldn't you? After all, we're all free agents. As I see it, it's not a thing that really comes within the scope of this meeting.' He looked round quickly, smiling a little with tight lips, anxious for approval.

Francisco said: 'One of the aims of our fraternity is to do our best to remedy injustice. Costa's been punished by us all, there's no use trying to close our eyes to the facts. But in my view there's a proper sentence for every crime and when that's been served a man goes free. Don't forget that Costa wasn't the only man in this village to have been caught in Fascist territory when the war broke out.'

'No,' a voice said, 'but he was the only one they thought enough of to decorate.'

'Took to it like a duck takes to water,' the man in a tight collar said, and Simón asked: 'What about that story you always hear about him taking one of our positions single-handed?'

'He's always denied it, and his word is as good as anybody else's.'

'What did he get the putty medal for then?'

'Well, what was it anyway? A merit cross, second class. They used to hand them out with the rations. The point is that no one can say that Costa hasn't toed the line since he came back here. Judge a man by his actions, I say.'

The grumbling chorus of disapproval had died down,

but Simón said: 'If he works on the boats, he'll be automatically eligible for membership of this fraternity. As that's so, may we have until next meeting to discuss the matter?'

'Very well,' said Francisco.

'It's a point we ought to bear in mind. But if it's all right with the others, I won't object.'

'Good,' Francisco said, 'and now we can get down to some serious business.'

There was a tap on the door and the old waiter was admitted, carrying a tray. Francisco took a glass of water and waited until the old man had gone out again. 'What I'm going to say now comes under our rule of total silence, wives included. Is that understood?'

Simón got up quietly and closed the window. Another of them opened the door and looked into the café, where a single customer, a ruined landowner dressed in mourning, was playing patience, and the old waiter had fallen asleep on his feet leaning against the cash register. He came in, closing the door softly, nodding to Francisco, and Francisco said: 'What I want to know is, what are we going to do about this new police lieutenant?'

CHAPTER 6

LIEUTENANT CALLES had exasperated the villagers by the excessive zeal of his enforcement of petty restrictions, and by his astonishing refusal to accept bribes had infuriated most of the rich, successful black-marketeers from Barcelona who retreated for the summer season to Torre del Mar. He had won renown in his service by crushing the smuggling industry at a local port in a ruthless campaign in which very questionable methods had been employed, and had then been sent to Torre del Mar to carry out a similar assignment. Had Calles not been a policeman, he would have liked to take holy orders, and enjoyed nothing better than to relax in his spare moments with a devotional manual.

On this particular afternoon, he had been embarrassed by the surprise visit of his colonel, whose personality had always remained for him an enigma.

The two men sat in comfortless chairs facing one another, the lieutenant stiffly upright and attentive and the colonel a little relaxed as befitted his rank. The colonel had placed himself where he could see the view through the window, which included some ramparts, the beach patched with rectangles of brown nets, and most of the bay with a barely covered reef showing pale through the water. Like a fault in an emerald, the colonel thought. But did emeralds have faults? Well, perhaps a crystal, then. He was a man of sensibility who, when in the company of his aristocratic cronies, affected deprecatory attitudes towards his profession. He had spent the last two years composing an eclogue of innumerable verses which still showed no signs of completion.

The colonel turned his attention to the lieutenant who sat there dummy-like, humourless and over-deferential, the skin of his pinkly new-shaven face already tightening into the mask of the ascetic. This room contained one deal table, two hard chairs, a religious picture shrilly coloured, a bed made up in army style. It smelt of a powerful disinfectant called Zotal.

'And how are we settling down in our little niche — nicely, I hope?' said the colonel. How tiresome it was that the requirements of rank made it impossible for one to unbend. He allowed himself another glance through the window. 'Idyllic,' he said. His eyes, which were weak, watered a little as if in appreciation. 'How I envy you!'

'I beg your pardon, sir?' Obediently, but with stolid distaste the lieutenant followed the colonel's gaze.

'I was referring to your delectable view,' said the colonel. He studied his subordinate; limited, narrow-minded, knowing little of the ways of men, honest enough — yes, a bit of a fanatic even. There were far too few of this kind for the purposes of the service, but, alas, too many for the good of humanity.

'You're satisfied with the way things are progressing with your duties?'

'I should never venture to describe myself as satisfied, sir. I've prepared a situation report here which you might care to glance at.' Calles eagerly opened a drawer in his desk and took out a file.

'We won't bother about the report for the moment,' the colonel said. 'Just give me the rough gist of it. Time's running short, and I should like to glance round the place before I go.'

'There's very little to trouble you with. Our only important case arose out of the big cache of contraband discovered last year.'

'I seem to remember something about it,' the colonel said, with a reluctant effort at concentration. 'Perhaps you'd refresh my memory.' Oh, God, how trivial it all was, he thought, measured in the scale of the eternal realities!

Colourlessly word-perfect, the lieutenant launched himself into the familiar recital. 'On the sixteenth of September at approximately fourteen hundred hours a young lady of foreign nationality who stated that she was searching for marine biological specimens entered a cave at Cala Blanca. At the extreme end of the cave she discovered a number of cases, one of which was open. She had the curiosity to examine the contents of this and found them to be birth-control requisites.'

'Surely not french letters?' asked the colonel, struggling with a smile.

'I'm afraid I'm unaware of the exact description of the articles in question, sir. In addition there were approximately five million cigarettes and various medicines.'

'It illuminates the national character,' the colonel said.

'I beg your pardon, sir?'

'I mean it demonstrates conclusively what we as a people require most of others.'

Calles looked back into space. 'As the result of our

investigations, fourteen persons were brought to trial, all local inhabitants. . . .'

'It's a tradition that never seems to die out,' the colonel said.

'. . . and a sentence of one month's imprisonment was awarded in each case.'

'Remarkably light, I should say.'

'Among those sentenced was a certain Euladio Castañas, who upon being released boasted in the presence of witnesses that he had had a very pleasant rest, and that, as "The Company" had paid four hundred pesetas a day prison-money, he couldn't grumble.'

'All very regrettable,' the colonel said. 'Discouraging, too, I should say. One asks oneself how on earth can they afford it.' He had taken out a packet of American cigarettes and was just about to offer them to the lieutenant, when he remembered and stuffed them back into his pocket.

'We weren't content to let the matter drop there, sir,' the lieutenant said. 'After several months' work we've unearthed a great deal of information which forms the body of my new report. For example, the man who paid out the prison-money and who, in fact, is the so-called company's local agent, happens to be our new mayor.'

'*Indeed*,' said the colonel, trying to stiffen the irreparable softness of his face with proper amazement.

'The contraband cargo, we discovered, came from Tangiers via Majorca, in the motorship *El Kasbah*, and the head of the company itself is . . .'

The colonel raised his hand. 'I know what you're going to say and I prefer it to remain unsaid.' He studied

Calles's face. 'I realize you're scandalized, lieutenant, but I want to remind you that your duty is mainly preventive, and investigatory only to a very limited degree.'

'Very well, sir.'

The Colonel began a familiar speech, for which his voice, acting upon its own authority, took on a slightly deeper, more resonant tone.

'Beware of an excess of zeal, lieutenant, and remember that here in Spain we are building the edifice of justice slowly and patiently with whatever materials we can lay our hands on. There aren't enough bricks to go round. If we knew too much it would break our hearts, any of us. Let's do our own duty as we see it, and leave others — particularly those who happen to be above us — to do theirs. Do you follow my reasoning?'

'Perfectly, sir.'

'Good. We're both of us cogs in a very rickety machine, lieutenant. It's the best our country can afford at present, so let's be content with being good reliable cogs, and not try to throw everything out of gear by being too clever.'

The colonel remembered another irritating matter that had to be dealt with. 'What's all this about the man Vilanova? He's nothing more than another of those senile old monarchists, as far as I can make out.'

'He exercises the worst possible influence on morale, sir. In particular, he makes statements in public which are interpreted as unfavourable to the regime, but as he's the biggest landowner for miles I felt unable to move without your instructions.'

The colonel reached over and took the paper which Calles was holding. 'Very old family, I see. Bound to have plenty of friends at court. What are we to do with him?'

'That depends on you, sir.'

'Well,' said the colonel, pleased to have found an excuse to see more of this delightful village, 'we'll make a start by paying him a little visit. Perhaps he'd be amenable to some quiet advice. We'd probably be saving ourselves trouble in the long run. Is there anything else on the agenda?'

'Not so far as I'm concerned, sir.'

'In that case, let's get down to something rather more important.'

He felt in his pocket, found a slip of paper, unfolded it and handed it to Lieutenant Calles. Calles found himself holding a leaflet, badly printed on thin, yellow paper.

'What's your opinion of that?' He was cheerfully dispassionate, like a philatelist displaying a not particularly interesting stamp.

Calles read: 'He hath put down the mighty from their seat and hath exalted the humble and meek.'

'About five thousand of those were handed out at a football match after the recent tramways strike,' the colonel explained.

'Dissemination of illegal propaganda, coming under article seven of the code relating to incitement to rebellion,' Calles rattled off mechanically. 'Within the scope of the military courts, of course.'

He looked at the leaflet again. 'By the wording and spelling I should say this has been drafted by a foreigner; illiterate, too.'

'Unfortunately not,' said the colonel. 'That is to say

the description foreigner wouldn't really be appropriate in the circumstances. They happen to be the words of the Mother of God, extracted from their biblical context.' The heavy, handsome, success-softened face had assumed an expression of humorous apology, as if in indulgence of a piece of sentimental irresponsibility on the part of some dear friend who was generally recognized to have gone a bit soft in the head. 'Of course, it isn't really of the slightest importance,' he said, 'but it does seem to irritate our superiors. I simply can't see why.'

Calles was shocked.

'The gentleman at the bottom of this little prank got away, back to France,' said the colonel. 'But our agents tell us he's coming back, and he'll be coming here, of all places. That means he'll be put ashore from a boat, one of these dark nights.'

'I don't think he'll get very far this time, sir.'

'Good,' said the colonel. 'We're expecting great things of you. You've got a big reputation to live up to.'

'Thank you, sir.'

'Try as I may,' the colonel said, 'I can't fathom the mentality of these people. We've smashed all they stood for in this country, they get nowhere, and all they achieve is a single miserable strike. We pick up nine out of ten of them within a day or two of crossing the frontier, they're disorganized, short of funds, ill-equipped and not very clever. And yet after thirteen years they still keep coming. I can't even begin to understand what's at the back of their minds. That is to say, I know what they're supposed to stand for, but why? I mean, what do they see in it? To go to a firing squad for that!'

The colonel had never been sincerer in his amazement. He was an ardent believer in accepting life just as it was. For him it had been a good life at the bottom, and all the way up, and still was, in its calm, sedate fashion, at the top. On the whole he was inclined to believe that in the rough-and-tumble of their existence, the generous, hungry, irresponsible poor had the best of it. But it was all good, and what kind of men could they really be who wanted to suppress this enthralling lottery, to stifle this life with its wantonness, its impostures, its savage drama, its charming unpredictability, in a soulless rectitude, so that in the end you were all no better off than a lot of ants? He thought there might be something to be said for exterminating such idiots, if for nothing else than to prevent healthy minded people from catching a disease that could do nothing but make them miserable.

The lieutenant was describing his security measures, the routine checks on householders, supervision of foreigners, road-blocks, restrictions of movement, while the colonel's attention played truant again, charmed by the gaiety of the view from the window, which included a curve of bay set with houses shining like small, very white teeth. Let's see, he thought, how does Azorín put it, writing of Cadiz? 'The rim of a silver cup', that's it.

He heard the lieutenant say: 'We promised to do our best to get her lover amnestied. She's proved very useful.'

'What's that?' the colonel asked.

'The gypsy informer,' Calles said. 'Her lover was mixed up in a wounding case. We've managed to put the screw on her to good effect. Working in the theatre, there's not much happens that she doesn't hear about.'

And there's the State for you, the colonel thought. At the top, the ceremonial parades, the diplomatic functions at El Pardo, the champagne-guzzling, the fancy uniforms and the fireworks, and at the bottom, holding it up, the dirty gypsy informers, and a collection of soulless oafs like our friend here. 'Have you any contacts among the people themselves?' he asked, 'I'm referring to the fisherfolk.'

Calles shook his head. 'They're closer than Moors. You can't do anything with them. Reds to a man at heart, although you can never get one of them to admit it, however much he's had to drink.'

'I may be able to help you,' the colonel said. He handed the lieutenant a slip of paper. 'Take a note of this name. It may prove to be of value. The man has a useful military record — with us, I mean. He may be just what you're looking for.'

CHAPTER 7

DON FEDERICO VILANOVA was breakfasting as usual, at ten-thirty, on a brick platform erected in a corner of his high-walled garden. His house was the highest in the village, the decayed remnant of a fortified farm in which his family had lived through two centuries of its steady decline. From where he sat Don Federico's eyes could range at will over five bays and three miniature peaks, and all that lay between them, extracting a delicate and incommunicable pleasure from such sights as that of a summer rivulet of black goats trickling down a dry watercourse, or the antics of a half-crazed maidservant in the house immediately below, dancing on the roof with clothes-pegs for castanets. To facilitate this amusement a pair of binoculars always stood within reach.

His handsome, middle-aged housekeeper, Maria, came up carrying the coffee through the garden that was full of chrysanthemums and emaciated cats, and Vilanova, watching her nervously, groped for his binoculars. Maria put down the coffee and stood there staring down at him with distaste, while Vilanova tried to absorb himself with all that was left of his universe that he wanted to see. Below him, brought absurdly near by the glasses, a fisherman was busy with a turtle, turning it over and passing a knife with a stealthy, almost intimate gesture round the inside of the shell, the water darkening with its blood. A foreign lady on the beach removed her dress, and with the slightest possible twinge of disappointment Don Federico observed that she was wearing a regulation bathing-costume beneath it. A sound that was half grunt, half cough, disturbed him, and reluctantly he turned away, brought back to earth by the knowledge that Maria was still standing there, sullen in dingy black, her slight moustache quivering with resentment.

'Well, what do you want to eat today?'

'Did Costa have any fish?'

'My dear man, if we were to wait for Costa's fish we'd wait a long time.'

Vilanova sighed. 'I've explained my attitude before. It's the only way in my power to demonstrate my sympathy with the struggle of the individual against the weight of blind social prejudice.'

'You can have your sympathy for lunch, then.'

'No,' said Vilanova. 'Bean stew for lunch and sympathy for supper. I'm better off with a light evening meal.'

'So it comes to this then, that I'm to be sacrificed to your weak stomach.'

'Make enough bean stew for both meals. You don't mind if I don't accompany you,' Vilanova said. 'Tell Costa to save us some fish on the next occasion. I'm all for the individual when he stands up to the herd. He can do it in the name of whatever he pleases.' He picked up the binoculars again, but Maria showed no signs of going.

'I want to speak to you seriously.'

Vilanova waved his hand. 'Some other time. Some other time.'

'You'll find you can't put me off like that. That woman was here last night again, wasn't she?'

Don Federico was pretending to manipulate the focusing wheel of his binoculars. 'A corrupt world, but how beautiful it can be!' he murmured.

'Well, answer me.'

'I've no intention of answering you,' Vilanova said. 'You're forgetting yourself.'

'Don't think it matters to me if you make a fool of yourself, but it might interest you to hear that the ormolu clock's gone, that's all.'

'Quite so,' Don Federico said, thinking quickly. 'I took it to be repaired.'

'You did nothing of the kind. You've been robbed, but your vanity won't let you admit it. Whatever else do you imagine a woman of her kind would want with an old rooster like you?'

'She's entirely right,' said Don Federico, voicing aloud, as he frequently did, a private reflection. 'What would she want? At my time of life the game's not worth the candle. There's nothing much left in love to disguise the basic bitter flavour.'

'Ave Maria purissima!' A voice reached them from below, just sufficiently loud to penetrate the buzzing of the bees over the surface of the wall. Don Federico looked down and saw the beggar with Parkinson's disease. 'Please go away,' he said to his servant, 'I don't want to scandalize our friend.' He leaned out over the wall. 'What did you say?'

The beggar repeated his greeting in a loud voice.

'That's better. I can't stick mumblers.'

Don Federico paid a peseta for the privilege of snapping at this beggar every morning. He took the peseta note from under a bottle. The beggar held up a stick, and Vilanova stuck the note in the cleft end.

'God will repay you,' said the beggar, again in a loud voice.

'Of course, of course.'

The beggar went away, waving his stick in salutation. The two of them were on the best of terms, and Don Federico regarded the beggar as an intelligent source of the information for which he affected to care nothing. He picked up a bell and tinkled it, and Juan, the half-wit who did the odd jobs, came out of the house.

'Get down the nest,' Vilanova told him.

Juan removed the metal collar that kept the cats from climbing the trunk of the almond tree, hoisted himself into its branches and brought down the nest with its five young birds. Vilanova gazed reverently at them, then spearing crumbs of bread with his toothpick he dropped one into each gaping, orange beak. 'Put them back again,' he told Juan. 'Really, I haven't the faintest idea what we're going to do about the cats when they grow their feathers and start flopping about.'

Vilanova had recovered from the nervous irritation of his encounter with Maria and was settling down to his enjoyment of a flawless day. The morning sounds were those of frogs and swifts; the frogs clucking cheerfully in innumerable wells — a sound identical with that made by a carter urging on his mules — and the swifts filling the sky with their squealings. Don Federico raised his cup, his bent finger roughly the colour and texture of the long-preserved china. A white splash of bird's droppings flecked the back of his hand, and he removed it tenderly with the corner of his napkin. How crystal-pure were the pleasures of the recluse! He had never regretted his withdrawal from the world, upon which it still entertained him to keep a sardonic eye. Suddenly his day went to pieces for, checking his binoculars in their sweep, he observed three figures on their way up the hill. What a bore! was his first reaction. Oh well, Maria can tell them I'm not at home. And then he recognized one of the men as his friend Doctor Rosas, from whom there would be no escaping, and what was worse he was accompanied by two men in police uniforms. Don Federico boiled with indignation. He detested all policemen on principle, and he was furious at Rosas's impertinence in daring to bring these men to his house.

'The wretches!' he said, speaking to himself aloud. 'After all, why should I put up with it? Just watch me send them packing.'

Half way up the hill Doctor Rosas's assurance deserted him. He became nervous. The mere presence of Calles was beginning to get on his nerves. It was impossible to relax for a moment with Calles. 'Of course, one has to bear in mind that the old chap's extremely eccentric. Cranky you might say. I don't know whether we'll get much sense out of him.'

The colonel said: 'I'm sure it's very good of you, doctor, to spare us your valuable time. I should have been sorry indeed to miss the opportunity of meeting your most prominent landowner. It's so rarely that I can get away to visit my territory.'

Rosas, who was already regretting his offer to present

thc colonel to his friend, said: 'I don't know that Vilanova won't strike you as being a pretty odd case. When you've known him a few years it's a different matter. The thing to remember is that basically he's one of the very best.'

'I'm sure of that,' the colonel said.

'Would you describe him, perhaps, as not being over-enthusiastic about the regime?' the lieutenant suggested, in a flat, professional voice, that sounded to the doctor too much like that of a cross-examining counsel.

'Oh good Lord, no! That's the very last thing I'd want to say!'

'Probably a bit of a hermit,' the colonel offered. 'Apt to tread on people's toes, I suppose.'

'Exactly,' Rosas said. 'Not to put too fine a point on it, he's a rude old man. Absolutely harmless, though. That's what I want to make clear. His wife died twenty years ago, and the son's a bit of a hot-head. Now he lives alone. More or less.'

'I hope Don Federico will understand the call's purely a courtesy one,' the colonel said.

'He'll be extremely gratified,' Rosas said. 'Even if he does appear to have a funny way of showing it. It's his manner that's difficult. Personally, I've learned how to handle him. My method is to keep cool and give him back as good as hc givcs. Hc understands that kind of treatment.'

'On the whole he sounds a rather delightful old character,' the colonel said. 'I'm quite looking forward to the experience.'

I only wish I could say the same, Rosas thought. If only I'd had some warning, I could have seen to it that he was out when they called. 'Oh, by the way,' he said, 'I forgot to mention something. Give him half a chance and he'll bore you to death with his ancestors. I thought I should warn you.' They both laughed, and Calles looked at them inquiringly.

'Well, that's one subject at least we shall have to keep off,' the colonel said.

CHAPTER 8

THEY were seated uncomfortably, facing each other on throne-like chairs in a huge half-empty room, in which grandiose pieces of furniture had been placed at random, as if waiting to come under the auctioneer's hammer. The walls were dark with damp-stains, and in several places brick showed through where the plaster had fallen away. Decades of silence had been entrapped and embalmed in the stagnant air between these walls.

The colonel had been admiring the details of Don Federico's face, that mask of dark, polished wood which scepticism and distrust had carved with their own tribal marks. Once again he tried a compliment. 'I really must congratulate you on your very handsome escritoire. It *is* a Louis XIV, is it not?'

'No,' said Vilanova. 'It's a vulgar provincial imitation from Madrid, but as Carlos the Third gave it to one of my ancestors I tolerate its presence.'

'We could live for a month on what we could raise on that old worm-trap,' Maria said. She had just come in and, braving Vilanova's frowns, had sat down resolutely on one of the thrones. The colonel, imagining her to be some kind of relation of Vilanova, was surprised that there had been no formal presentation.

Vilanova turned to her. 'Would it be too much to ask you to serve a glass of rancio?'

Maria got up and went out muttering.

Rosas leaned over to the colonel and whispered: 'That's his girl friend.'

'I see,' the colonel whispered back.

A rickety chicken staggered into the room, collapsed, righted itself. 'Hold up there, darling,' Vilanova cried imploringly. 'Really I don't know. I give them the best of everything. Perhaps it's the heat.' He was speaking more to himself than to the company.

'You may well be right,' said the colonel, conscientiously urbane. 'It can be most trying, although speaking for myself I don't find it excessively hot for the time of the year.'

'I couldn't agree with you less,' Vilanova said. 'Like everything else, the weather's gone to the dogs.'

Maria had returned unnoticed and resumed her seat. 'I can remember in the days when we *did* have summers when it rained for a week at a time,' she said. Her face was absent at the memory of a childhood made up of the cool days of spring and autumn with the beautiful dove-grey of overcast skies, and a little rain falling.

'And the rancio?' Vilanova said. 'Where's the rancio?'

'We've run out.'

'Well give them something, confound them!' said Vilanova in an undertone heard by all present. 'Get some white wine, and try to see to it that there are no mice in the barrel this time.'

The housekeeper flounced out of the room, but was back almost immediately and the colonel found himself holding a handsome goblet with a little clouded wine in its bottom, which he sipped doubtfully.

Rosas was trying to involve Calles in the conversation.

'And how do you like life in Torre del Mar, lieutenant?'

'My personal tastes don't enter into the matter,' Calles said in a tone of voice which contained a trace of schoolmasterly reproof.

The colonel groaned inwardly and Vilanova looked up interested.

Rosas struggled on. 'But surely you . . . well, let's say, approve of the place, in a general manner of speaking?'

'No,' said Calles, 'I don't. But then, I repeat, in the service, personal feelings aren't of the slightest importance.'

'The climate I suppose?' suggested Rosas weakly.

'No, the people,' Calles said, steadfastly avoiding the colonel's efforts to catch his eye.

'Thank God at least for someone who's not a born liar!' Vilanova said.

'Oh, come now, lieutenant,' the colonel said, 'Surely there are good and bad to be found everywhere.'

'They're irreligious here, sir. That's the trouble,' Calles said. 'They're the one exception in my experience throughout the Peninsula to the movement back to God.'

'Rubbish!' Vilanova said.

'I beg your pardon?' Calles asked. He was not sure whether or not Vilanova's remark was intended for the audience.

'I said rubbish.'

Calles went pink. 'I gather you overlooked the long article by Font in last Tuesday's *Vanguardia*. You would have found it of quite exceptional interest.'

'It's ten years since I last opened a newspaper; a beggar who comes up here every day tells me any news that's worth hearing.'

'The author mentioned a number of remarkable occurrences. You've heard of the case only last month of the peasants who discovered sacred relics under a waterfall?'

At this point Rosas, who had at last thought of a way of changing the conversation, tried to cut in, but Don Federico plunged on, unheeding. 'And what bearing do you suppose that has on the matter?'

'I regard it as a sign of the times,' said the lieutenant.

There was a background of woolly, distorted music from a small radio-set by the window which Don Federico kept permanently switched on while he was in the garden, not because he liked to listen to it but because it stimulated a nightingale, invisible among the unkempt bushes. In desperation Doctor Rosas now reached this and increased the volume. Through the blurred electrical sounds he could still hear Don Federico saying: 'On the whole I agree with you. And where did this extraordinary event take place?'

'Very near the place where I was born. A few miles from Pamplona.'

Rosas twirled the tuning dial, the radio chirped and whistled, the nightingale in the garden responded with a brief burst of notes. Vilanova said: 'It's several centuries since we staged that kind of fraud in Catalonia.'

There was embarrassed silence.

'I say it's several centuries since we staged that kind of fraud in Catalonia.'

'We all heard you,' Maria said from the back of the room.

'In that case, well and good. I wasn't sure whether my remark was sufficiently audible.'

'Our friend comes from an old dissenting family,' said Rosas appealingly. There was no longer any hope of saving the situation, so the old man might as well be given the cue for his usual speech. All newcomers to Torre del Mar were treated to it sooner or later.

'We've a long tradition of non-participation,' Don Federico explained. 'Half our family was wiped out by the Inquisition of Seville over a matter of a Latin grammatical construction in one of the articles of faith. Since then we don't take these things so seriously.'

Rosas wanted to wink at the colonel, but the colonel was looking away.

'You're dealing with fishermen here,' Vilanova said, 'and I'll tell you what to expect of them. They're God-fearing, but I suppose you're right when you say they're irreligious, if by that you mean they don't go in for kissing images' toes. The Church lost its last chance here when it forced them to go to Mass after the civil war. They've got no reason to like governments, or political parties — or the police.'

Just listen to the old fool, Rosas thought. He's cooking his goose this time.

'How interesting,' said the colonel gently. 'Am I to gather you're more or less of the same opinion?'

'You might say that,' Don Federico agreed.

The colonel looked at him almost tenderly. What a splendid old fellow after all, a real dyed-in-the-wool anarchist surviving like a solitary mastodon in a modern world. The colonel would have liked to establish a reserve for such human rarities where they could be kept comfortably out of mischief. And to think he had made the fatal mistake of bringing this oaf of a lieutenant along. The fool might even dare to put in a report over his head. Well, it was too late to do anything about it now, beyond perhaps softening the blow.

He got up and held out his hand to Vilanova. 'It's been most interesting to meet you. Be sure I envy your charming window on the world up here.'

'At least the only corruption I can smell comes from my neighbour's rubbish dump,' Vilanova said. 'And that's not so bad.'

Still smiling, the colonel murmured a quotation from Fray Luis de León in praise of the solitary life. He nodded to Calles who was standing as stiffly as if on parade. Rosas, seeing them to the door, excused himself from accompanying them down to the village. 'I believe the old fellow wants to consult me professionally.' 'Of course, of course,' said the colonel, and Rosas wondered why he found his affability a little chilling.

When he came back into the room Don Federico got up, and without a glance in his direction walked past him and went to a cabinet which contained the remnants of a fine collection of Sèvres porcelain. Selecting an exquisite saucer, he placed it on a side table. He then took off his coat and hung it on the back of a chair, half filled a washbasin from a pitcher and, taking out his false teeth, laid them tenderly in the saucer. Rosas, who had settled himself in one of the carved thrones, looked on grinning.

Suddenly Don Federico, who was now furiously lathering his chin, turned round. 'I see you can't take a hint.'

'You don't mean you want to get rid of me?'

'That's what it looks like, doesn't it?'

'I can't understand why. It's days since we had the opportunity of a chat.'

Vilanova replaced his teeth. 'You're devoid of all decency. Having forced your way into this house with those two monsters, you might at least have had the delicacy to clear off when they did.'

'Don't be an old idiot,' Rosas said. 'I was only acting in your own interest. You'd have made an even bigger ass of yourself than you did if I hadn't come along to keep an eye on you. Heaven knows you put your foot into it badly enough.'

'Do you find it extraordinary that I like to speak my mind in my own house?'

'In the circumstances, very,' Rosas said.

'That's because you're a confirmed hypocrite.'

'A play-actor, I prefer to say. You may live to regret not being one yourself. Anyway, let's change the subject. Here's the stuff I promised to get you the other day.'

Reluctantly Don Federico took the small packet and examined it from several angles.

'What's this?'

'For your cough.'

Vilanova ripped the cellophane off the packet, opened one end, and extracted a small bottle. Unscrewing the top, he shook a black pellet into the palm of his hand.

'And might I inquire what this nostrum consists of?'

'Vitamins, among other things,' Rosas said. 'I'm trying a new approach, although I'm well aware that you'd probably prefer a nice old-fashioned bottle full of foul-tasting liquid.'

Don Federico carefully replaced the black pill; then, taking the packet delicately between finger and thumb, held it out to Rosas. 'Sorry, not in the least interested. Witchcraft of any kind leaves me cold.'

'Oh, come now . . .' Rosas started.

'There's a pig-castrater I know, who follows the fairs, who deals in the self-same article. Recommended for everything from delayed menstruation to falling hair. Vitamins, indeed. What swindle will they think of next?'

'I suppose you'd like me to bleed you,' Rosas said. He was enjoying himself. At last he had found out how Vilanova was to be handled.

'By all means, if I thought you had any idea of how to go about it. Your father had a very good name for his blood-letting. He was noted for the cleanness of his incision.'

'That was my grandfather. My father always recommended enemas and lemonade.'

'But both of them better doctors than you. They tell me that you're filling the new cemetery even more quickly than they filled the old, and also that they're calling you Dr. Seduction these days.'

Rosas's smile went stiff. 'And I hear that you're being unfaithful to your housekeeper with a tart from the theatre.'

Vilanova glanced round nervously, and then returned to the attack, happy at last in the knowledge that he had penetrated the doctor's defences. 'Look here, Rosas . . . natural charlatanism apart, do you really think that vitamin pills are going to cure my cough?'

'No,' said Rosas.

'Of course you don't. Then why should you expect me to?'

'The medicine that can cure your cough doesn't exist.'

'Well, I even prefer to hear that than to be taken for a moron.'

'Nothing can cure your cough,' said Rosas, his mouth still imprisoned in the tight smile, 'because you haven't one. Not as recognized by medicine. You have a psychological device for drawing attention to yourself. Not a cough in any real sense. You have no cough.'

'And I suppose I want to draw attention to myself even when I'm alone?' Now he had scored his hit, Vilanova felt his good humour returning. His tone became more indulgent.

'Even when you're alone. A psychological device, not a true cough. You're old, my friend, and it appears that some of us when we get old can't find anything better to do than to get up to these tricks to draw attention to ourselves.'

Vilanova's mouth opened and closed again. Suddenly he could think of nothing to say, and at the same moment he felt every cranny of his inner life illuminated by a cruel, brilliant light. For the briefest instant he saw himself objectively, a pathetic stranger; accepting humbly, without question, a preposterous revelation. He felt almost faint with melancholy. All the flamboyance of his youth, the folly and the bravado, the foolish glittering panoply of cherished memories: a cave gypsy in a Paris gown brazenly, defiantly paraded through the salon of the Duquesa de la Calatrava, a gondola on the Manzanares, an episode in the bullring of Huelva which had cost him three weeks in hospital and a fine of a thousand pesetas — all this generous ostentation had sickened and died, leaving only, as a kind of ghost of itself, a dry cough in an old man's throat.

Somewhere above in the woods, a woodpecker laughed suddenly, and the sad and foolish sound came to them through the open window.

'There's nothing wrong with you,' said the doctor, 'that isn't bred in your own imagination. To tell you the truth, you also cough because you're choking in a sense of your own futility. You see your life coming to its end and, inside you, you realize how little you've done with it.'

'Yes,' said Vilanova, who had suddenly sunk down in a chair. 'That's true.'

'By God,' Rosas said, 'don't you think I've had enough of treating *malades imaginaires* such as you. You're out of joint with the times, and what have you ever done about it except bluster? Nothing, my dear chap. And now, as you can't take it out on anybody else, you're taking it out on me with your imaginary ailments.'

He waited for the counter-attack, but none came. Vilanova sat there in silence, shaking his head.

Down in flames, Rosas said to himself. One good broadside and he's finished. But now that his own fury was relieved there was shame in his triumph.

'I'm going,' he said. He got up and patted Vilanova on the shoulder, suddenly penitent. 'Sorry, old man. I let my tongue run away with me. See you down at the Twentieth Century some time — eh?'

Vilanova did not answer.

CHAPTER 9

THE colonel's car awaited him at the entrance to the village and there he and Calles parted company, the colonel to be swept reluctantly away to the insipid routine that lay in wait for him in the city, and Calles to embark on his fretful daily patrol of the fishing village which he detested so much.

The first thing that Calles saw to irritate him was a boat which had been repainted and renamed *Inteligencia.* Faintly the old name *Milagros* could still be seen beneath the new coat of yellow paint. Calles called a boy over. 'Who's the owner of that vessel?'

'Francisco.'

'Francisco who?'

'I don't know, just Francisco.'

Calles made a note of the name in his mental black book. Miracles and Intelligence. This incident typified for him the vulgar, self-satisfied shallowness of the Mediterranean, which rejected the mysterious perfection of the divine, in favour of the crude fallibility of man. He glanced at the names of some of the other boats. *Venus, Happy, Girls at Home.* There they were, lolling and sluttish on the beach, stinking of the putrid fat used to grease the rollers, and behind them the sea was like a vacant face.

The lieutenant detested the sea, its placid boredom, its treachery, and the false affability of those who lived by it, these men of shallow smiles and hidden minds, squanderers of the riches the ocean showered on them, atheists. Even more he detested the smug heartlessness of the village, with its neglected church, where there was no silent, dignified, fore-ordained poverty, and no wealth either that he could respect, like that, for example, of his homeland, Navarra, where the rich and poor were two equally valuable and indispensable aspects of a divine order — both of them bound to the soil and to God. Here the rich were unnecessary, an empty and meaningless presence, isolated in their ugly houses. And most of them malefactors who had covered up their misdeeds.

In this place, thought the lieutenant, they bought and sold men. They had bought his predecessor and destroyed him, and soon they would try to buy him, too. Corruption had come in with prosperity. Who had prospered here? Why, the corrupt, as everybody knew. And on what had all those vulgar palaces that defaced the hillsides been built but bribe-taking and the manipulation of food supplies in the days when half the nation had starved? Corruption — in that respect the old monarchist had been right. All the men who had built these houses, mixing blood with the mortar, were charming men. Calles had met them all. Corruption was hospitality, it was a sense of humour, it was devotion to one's family, it was christening presents for poor children and a little charity done in public. This was the real enemy. This was what compromised justice, blackened the name of religion, separated the classes, kept twenty million Spaniards licking their wounds unreconciled.

Lieutenant Calles came into the village main street, which was very narrow. There was a fish-market in this street and, catching a reek of fish, of which the whole village stank so badly, he closed his nostrils, nauseated, and breathed through the mouth.

In the length of the street there were three bars and a few fishermen were going into them and coming out. Calles had turned it into a one-way street several weeks before. At the far end of it, narrow as a ravine, he saw his sergeant, back to him, also on his way to the police-station.

A large, new American car, of the kind which Calles knew could only be had by a big-scale black-market operation, entered the street, coming in the wrong direction, passed the sergeant and came feeling its way and bleating softly towards him. The car was being driven very slowly. It was obliged to stop at the fish-market while a stall was moved to allow it to pass. The fish-wives were very polite, laughing and waving their hands to whoever was in the car. Just before the car reached Calles, he stepped out into the road.

'Are you aware that this is a one-way street?'

A chauffeur in green livery was driving, and a pretty, fair-haired woman, who was unmistakably a very high-class whore from Barcelona, sat in the back. The woman, who wore a ridiculous little black hat, smiled at him. The chauffeur seemed very surprised. 'Sorry, sir, I won't make the mistake again.'

'Back up,' Calles said.

The chauffeur glanced back at the woman, who was still smiling. 'It's a bit difficult, sir. There's only an inch or two's clearance for the wheels on each side.'

'Back up,' Calles said again.

'All the way?'

'All the way,' Calles said.

The pretty lady threw up her hands, eyes rolling. Calles didn't know her, but he knew the car. It belonged to a genial crook universally known by his first name, Alfonso. He watched the car back painfully up the street, tyres squealing as they were forced against projecting stones. It took ten minutes to cover a hundred yards, Calles following till it was out of the street.

He then went straight to the police-station, and called the sergeant to his office.

The sergeant came and stood to attention in front of his desk, a puffy, empty, middle-aged face, with weak eyes, and a dirty boil-plaster on his neck.

'All right, stand easy,' Calles said. 'I called you to refresh my memory. What happened last week when the charcoal-burner drove his cart in the wrong direction up the one-way street?'

'If you'll pardon the expression, sir, we tickled his ribs.'

'Oh,' said Calles.

'He couldn't pay a fine,' said the sergeant, not liking Calles's eye, moistening his lips.

'Why did you let that car pass just now?'

'I was too late to stop it, sir. He was already half way up the street.'

'You should have made him back,' Calles said. 'In future you will do so, and what is more you will arrest the chauffeur of that particular car if he tries it again.'

'Very well, sir.'

'And now before you go, I want to talk to you about harbour regulations. I saw a stranger out in one of the fishing-boats today. Has the ruling that boats may carry only their registered crews been rescinded?'

'Not officially, sir.'

'Well, in future, regulations will be respected until they're officially rescinded. I'm going to make these people toe the line.'

The sergeant sighed inwardly. 'Does that apply to summer visitors, sir?'

'It goes for everybody.'

Calles waved the man away, then called him back. 'What's this?' He had just noticed a large, shapeless brown-paper parcel lying across his desk. He tore open an end, and both men saw the brownish fur of some animal.

'A hare, sir. I understand it's a gift from Martinez of the cork factory.'

'Take it away and bury it,' Calles said.

CHAPTER 10

MOLINA arrived on the two-thirty bus next afternoon, having travelled by train second class from Perpignan to Gerona, where he had spent an hour buying various parts necessary to convert his portable radio-set to a transmitter. Molina was dressed in a French suit, carried a French passport, and spoke Spanish with a slight French swallowing of the r's. This was to be expected because he had lived in France since, as a boy of eighteen, he had been a human particle in that avalanche of hopeless, famished, terror-stricken refugees, pouring over the eastern Pyrenean frontier. But now, suddenly, having become almost a complete Frenchman, premature middle-age had turned him with one tap of its malevolent wand into one of those figures of bone and dark parchment who are to be seen leading their mules through any jagged village in the Spanish landscape. A Spaniard of the Spaniards.

Molina's luggage on this, one of many return visits, included a folding easel, a box of paints with a false bottom and a tiny phial containing two cyanide pills. He was still a little queasy from the succession of Pernods which he had felt obliged to drink while the Customs formalities dragged on in their interminable way at Port-Bou.

At the Miramar Hotel Molina found that all the fourteen rooms had already been taken, but the porter obligingly offered to find him accommodation in the village, and at the third attempt they found a house with a room to let that suited him. It was a bare white-washed, prison-like chamber under the roof, reached by a step-ladder at the end of a passage, and with it went the use of the roof-terrace, and the enjoyment of a tremendous panorama, which Molina failed to notice.

As soon as the old woman went out of the room and began her laborious, creaking descent, Molina dropped down on the bed and, with eyes closed tried to calm his nerves. He was a spent volcano, old before his time, and at last he was sure of it. Molina had been one of those born to give themselves to a cause, any cause that would put to work the enthusiasm they generate as if by a bodily process. And now these well-springs had suddenly failed. The genius for seeing things in high contrast had dried up. Once it had been all certainty — black and white, right and wrong, hero and beast; but now treacherous half-tones had invaded the picture. There was only one treatment for this disease, which Molina knew was no more than decay of the tissues masking itself under a comfortable, rational form. That was tighter and tighter self-discipline, the establishment of an ever stricter dictatorship over his faltering resolve. It became necessary to go on believing, because the other way led to the terrible knowledge that his life had been thrown away, that all the struggles and the sacrifice had been for nothing. But somewhere within him Molina knew that a personal fifth-column was at work, and as a result nothing he did was done as it would have been done had the enthusiasm and the conviction still been alive. He was becoming third-rate. He would carry this job through. But for the sake of the others, if for no other reason, he knew it must be the last.

At thirty-two, Molina the worn-out veteran was the only survivor of his revolutionary group. He had constantly recurring nightmares about his last mission when all had gone well — almost too well — until they were on their way back, and then when ten miles past Besalu and almost at the foot of the pass, nervously happy and betrayed into a false confidence, the searchlights had suddenly come on, lighting up the valley like daylight. He would never forget the screams of his comrades as the bullets hit them, and the terrible yelping of the frontier-guards' dogs as they were freed from their leashes. Now, of course, it had been recognized — too late, as usual — that all the passes were out of the question, and that any arms, equipment, or propaganda material, would have to be brought in by sea. So Molina, whose inner collapse remained unsuspected, had been sent to report on the coastal security precautions, and to discover, if possible, a suitable spot for the landing of a small party.

There was a tap on the door, and the old woman was there to know if he wanted anything to eat. Molina told her ungraciously that he wanted to be left in peace. Then, controlling himself quickly, he called her back.

'Señora, I was wondering. Do you happen to know anybody with a boat. I'd like to go out fishing tomorrow.'

'You've come to the right place for that,' she said. 'My son will be able to fix you up. Any time you like to make it. He'll be back tonight and you'll be able to talk to him yourself.'

Next day Costa took Molina out in the boat. He was apologetic because they had been unable to make an early start. 'I had an appointment with a fish, but it didn't show up.' He told Molina about the big merou and the long, fruitless excursion he had made that morning, setting out before dawn. 'You need plenty of patience at this job. Tomorrow, or the next day, or the day after that. I'm not pushed for time.'

Molina nodded absently.

'You won't catch anything to shout about this time of day,' Costa said. 'The morning's better.'

'We'll make it the morning next time then.'

'What do you want to fish for?' Costa asked.

'I don't know. Anything.'

'The point is that to catch anything worth having you have to go into deep water. I know a reef a mile or two off-shore where we could try for bream. Even then, it's the wrong time of day.'

'Let's stick to the shore,' Molina said. 'Isn't there anything in all those bays?' From where he sat in the stern he could see the headlands jutting out of ten miles of coastline, the nearest a dark and solid red, and then by degrees greying and paling, until the farthest was a mist-filled shape, enclosed by a wavering pencilled line at the sky's base.

'The only rock fish you can catch with a line,' Costa said, 'are serrans. They're about the size of your finger. Your little finger. You'd have to catch twenty or thirty of them to make a meal.'

'I'd like to see something of the coast,' Molina said. 'We'll go out to the reef next time.'

'You're hiring the boat,' Costa said. 'There's nothing wrong with serrans if you can catch enough of them. But, if it's worth-while fish you're after, you've got to go out into deep water.'

Molina said, 'Serrans will do. Let's try over there by those caves.'

Costa pulled on his oar and the boat turned shorewards. They covered a hundred yards in silence, Costa's face turkey-red in the full glare of the sun. Small, glistening globes of perspiration formed at the roots of his thin hair and trickled down the shining skin of his forehead. Molina's gaze was over Costa's shoulder, scanning the crumbling rampart of cliffs.

'Might as well start here,' Costa said. 'It's as good here as anywhere.'

He left the oars to trail in the water and came back to rummage in the space under the stern for the lines. He found a line wound on a thick wedge of cork, with a spacer and three hooks. A tentacle of a small dead octopus curled out from under a floorboard, and Costa bent down, and cut it off with his clasp-knife.

Molina watched the shore.

'Better show you the way we bait up,' Costa said.

Molina forced himself to produce a show of interest in the procedure.

'For instance, plenty of fish wouldn't so much as look at a hook with the smell of your hands on it. Serrans are different. They're greedy feeders.'

'Gently with the line, now,' Costa said, 'or you'll lose your bait. There we go. Just look at all those fish down there. There must be a thousand of them. You can see them bobbing the hooks about with their noses.' Somebody to talk to, once in a while, Costa thought. It makes all the difference. He hoped Molina would want to come out fishing every day.

Molina peered into the depths, but saw nothing but a few feet of wavering line, the pale rocks under the surface shifting stealthily, yellow-meshed with filtered sunlight, set in a green void. Then even this unsubstantial vision of another world was cancelled in a wash of reflections of cliff-top, cloud and sky.

'What's the use spending a fortune on fancy tackle? You've got to know what goes on in a fish's mind. When you feel a nibble, give the line a good jerk . . . Here, let me show you the way to do it.'

Costa reached out for the line and took it delicately between thumb and finger. Molina watched him for a moment, the sun-flayed disappointed face, the fair hair as coarse as coconut fibre on the freckle-blotched arms. He tried to think of something to say.

'Take them by surprise,' Costa said. 'That's how we do it.' The line came up quickly, dripping water, with two small brightly enamelled fish on the hooks, twisting their bodies and opening and closing transparent sail-like fins.

Costa chopped three more slivers from the octopus tentacle, baited the hooks, and handed back the line. Molina took it absently and settled himself more comfortably against the gunwale. The boat, drifting, had come round slowly so that the sunshine now prickled on his cheek and on the pale, dry skin of his right arm. Over on the other side, away from the sun, he could still see the shore, but somehow it seemed now as if it was less urgent to look, as if the rocking of the boat had produced an hypnotic effect.

Here the cliffs were the colour of a lion skin with every spur whitened where peregrines had perched. Molina heard the faint cough of the water as it moved in and out of distant caves. He felt slightly drugged, and with this feeling a sensation of wonder like that of a patient on the operating table surprised by the insidious power of an anaesthetic. Molina, who had lived in the kernel of an obsession and therefore half oblivious to the physical world around him, felt in these surroundings a momentary peace and security. For a brief moment the external would come close to him, focused in a thousand re-awakened sensations, while inner realities of his own making became vaporous and unimportant. At that instant he would have asked nothing better than to change places with this fisherman, to live a warm, satisfying animal life, with little, regular successes cancelling out the regular failures, and nothing more important than the satisfaction of bodily needs.

A thin babel of echo-less voices coming across the water broke into his thoughts. Molina's eyes came into focus. Seawards, perhaps a mile away, the smooth water swelled up round a reef, withdrew it from sight, then lazily thrust it forth, like the tip of a blackened tongue. All round the reef were the tiny shapes of boats, two men in each. He could see these black-silhouetted manikins on their feet in the boats, gesticulating. These men seemed to be engaged in a desperate battle with some unseen enemy.

'The tunny shoal,' Costa explained. 'They've caught up with the shoal at last. Never know where they're going to show up next. If you can manage to stay with the shoal for a day or two, you can coin money. Make enough to keep things going for half the summer.' Molina caught the expression of envy.

'Why don't you catch some yourself?'

'I'm on my own. For the tunny you need two in the boat. One has to be free to play the fish while the other manages the boat. What with keeping fresh water running through the live-bait and winding up the lines, he has his hands full enough.'

'I see,' said Molina.

Out at sea the confusion increased as the big fish took the hooks, towed the boats in circles, tangled the lines, toppled the fishermen into the water. The men yelled with anguish as the nylon cut into their bleeding hands.

'Some of those fellows ought to learn how to fish,' Costa said, but the excitement had infected him. 'You know, the fact is it's not so easy. The line goes out at a hundred kilometres an hour. You can't hold it. Just leave it to unwind itself. Makes a row like a whip-lash. You've got to know what you're doing. I've known a fellow's finger taken off clean.'

The distant clamour had died down. 'The shoal's passed,' Costa said. He felt happy that the others' luck had been so short-lived. 'Better pull your line in,' he said. 'You've got something there.' He took two more serrans off the hooks and tossed them into the bottom of the boat. Out there they had been catching tunny, while he had been fishing like a schoolboy for serrans. The humiliation rankled.

'Let's try the next bay,' Molina said.

To reach the next bay they had to pass a low headland which was the colour of rust and shaped like some sea-monster with a despairing mouth. A few pines crammed their bare roots into its crevices and a single seagull with a big yellow bill balanced on the highest point. Molina smelt the pine-needles heaped in the rock-crevices, sun-roasted, and the scent of cistus and frigola coming from the beautiful barren land over the cliff behind. Round the headland the boat nosed into a polished lagoon, with the water heavy as the oars sliced into it, showing first plum-stained from the weed below, then clear green-white over the sand. A cataract of vegetation, forced down a tight ravine, had fallen and dried at the back of the beach as salt worked through the sand around the tenacious roots. There were a few planks on the sand, white-fibred, with water-smoothed edges.

'There doesn't seem to be a beach-shack here,' Molina said.

'The old fellow who owns the property won't stand for it,' Costa said. 'He can't stop people picnicking, but he's within his rights in not letting them put up a shack.'

'Can you get up to the road from here?'

'There's a path, but it's pretty much overgrown. Smugglers used to land their stuff here in the old days before they fixed the police. Now they bring it ashore in the harbour in broad daylight. At least, they used to until someone gave the show away, and the lieutenant got five years.'

Molina said: 'I feel like a bit of exercise. You may as well put me ashore here, and I'll walk back. First I might have a swim.'

'Mind the current,' said Costa.

* * *

After the tunny shoal had passed, the fishermen rowed on stealthily, talking in low tones, sniffing the air. The fishermen credited the fish with acute senses, particularly those of smell and hearing. They also believed that many of their own number could smell the shoals of fish as they passed beneath in the water. Celestino, who had been proved most successful in such matters, led the crescent of boats. He was assisted by his son Juan whose task it was to control the flow of fresh sea-water through the boat by constantly removing and replacing the drain-plug, and baling out. The sand-eels used for bait became torpid in a few minutes if left in standing water.

'Look over there,' Juan said in a low voice.

'Over where?'

'There.'

Celestino screwed his head round and saw Costa's boat under the cliffs. He eased the pull on the oars to shrug his shoulders.

'Bad luck,' Juan said.

'You make your own luck, good or bad,' Celestino said. 'Anyway, you may as well get used to the sight of Costa, because he'll probably be with us next time we take the big boat out.'

'Who said so?'

'Francisco.'

'You can tell Francisco to go and . . .'

'Don't talk like that—in front of your father, at any rate.' Celestino sniffed suddenly with widened nostrils, and expression withdrawn. Catching at some faint trick of sensation that had come and gone in an instant. 'Throw out more bait,' he said.

Juan dropped the baling can, reached down and scooped up a handful of the sluggish sand-eels drifting about in the water over the sand, and flung them out as far as he could behind the boat. Then he snatched up one of the lively fish which had burrowed under the sand so that just the pointed snout and eyes protruded, hooked it smartly through the lower part of the body, and threw the line after the bait. Both men watched the line for perhaps a minute. 'Pull in,' Celestino said. He gestured towards the shore. 'They went across that way.'

'What do you expect?' Juan said. 'Do you expect any luck with him about?'

'In my young days only old women talked like that. It goes to show the kind of education you get. All you kids are a bit soft in the head.'

'Well, I don't like his face, then,' Juan said.

'Bale out, and keep baling out. And don't forget that Costa's a good fisherman. A better fisherman than you'll ever be. A good man to have in any boat.'

Celestino rowed on, his oars cutting the surface silently, with the precision of lancets. 'We're over them again,' he said. 'Try not to get excited and tread on the fish.'

Juan threw out another handful of bait and followed it with the line. Celestino felt the presence of the shoal very strongly now. He shipped his oars, listening to the spatter of the bait hitting the water, and the flat, clean, sea-washed sounds from the other boats; the oars straining on their ropes, and the quick splash of the men baling-out. And then, just when he was going to tell Juan to pull in again, he heard the warning shout from one of the farthest boats, and flinging himself forward on his knees in the sand and water he caught up the second line, baited the hook and threw it out. At that moment, just as the men in all the boats shouted together, the fish struck at both hooks and the seventy-five-gauge nylon line wound on the thick cork centres that lay free by the gunwales went out in great, whipping snatches, thirty feet at a time with the corks bouncing and spinning in the air.

In the moment of the shoal's passing every boat had hooked one or two fish, and now the tunny were towing the boats in all directions. Some boats were circling out of control, others about to ram each other, with the fish in the first freshness and fury of their will to escape, and the men fighting to hold them at the bottom of their tremendous dives with only a few feet of line left in the boat, and then winding in the line as quickly as ever they could as the fish came soaring back to the surface, baling out the boat between dives, rowing after the fish, avoiding by hairbreadths collisions with other boats, cutting-free tangled lines, screaming curses and threatening each other, falling asprawl in the water in their boats, and overbalancing to topple into the sea.

Peering through the twisting reflections, Celestino saw the lifeless aluminium shape of the tunny they had hooked, its sheen slaked in blue water, going by on its side in its slow circuit of the boat. Far below, the shoal still passed, a comet's tail of streamlined metal and, snatched from this shooting motion, the small silver kite of the fish on Juan's line, straining into the intense blue.

On its third circuit of the boat the fish had almost reached the surface. Celestino transferred the line to his left hand, took the gaff in his right, and with a sudden jerk of the line steered the fish in towards the boat. Now came the supreme moment of the fisherman's art as he struck down with the gaff, hooking the fish in the tough skin over the backbone, and with a jerk and a lift bringing it up on to the gunwale, balancing it there for a moment, then crashing it down into the boat. There it lay, red-black blood rivulets on its polished surfaces draining into the water while Celestino roped it by the tail before swinging it up on to the decked-over stern. Out of the water the fish had become a life-sized child's toy, rigid and unconvincing, with tinny head and jaws, its sides a little brassy through the plating, and straight grooved lines fanning out from the corners of the mouth across cheek and eyeball, where the fish had been held fighting, head down, at the bottom of its dives.

Celestino unhooked the line, rebaited it and threw it back, hearing at that moment Juan's fish come into the boat with a great splash behind him. Juan manhandled his catch into position beside Celestino's fish, and roped up the tail. He rebaited his hook and threw out the line. Both men were spattered with the tunnies' dark blood and the water in the bottom of the boat had turned pink. Juan took out the plug and the water gushed in. He did not bale out now because they believed that the fish would be frightened off by the scent of blood in the water. Two minutes passed, while silence settled down again in all the boats. 'May as well take in the lines and bale out,' Celestino said. 'The shoal's passed.' He dabbed a little petrol on his hands where the old line cuts had opened again, and took up the oars.

'Should we circle round a bit and try to pick it up?' Juan asked.

'We'll keep going to the Cabra, and then turn round,' Celestino said. 'They won't come back this way.'

'What's the weight of the fish?' he asked.

'About eighty kilos,' Juan said. 'That's a hundred and forty with the first couple we took.'

'That's not bad,' Celestino said. 'Pretty good fishing. We were talking about Costa just now. Costa would have caught two fish in the time it took you and me to catch one. That would have been better still.'

'I don't see how he could.'

'Well, he would have. He'd have kept two lines going at once. *And* he wouldn't have crossed them. So if either of us had been rowing with Costa in the boat we'd have six fish now, instead of four.' Celestino had decided that only facts like this were likely to appeal to a generation of materialists. You talked to them through their pockets or their stomachs.

'We could catch a lot more fish with Costa in the big boat,' he said. 'If anybody's going to take him on, it might as well be us.'

CHAPTER 11

JUST before dawn a small, moaning wind arose, sweeping the cock-crows out of the hills into the village, and the men knew that there would be no fishing that day. This gave Costa an opportunity to make a trip in to Barcelona.

For days his alarm over Elena's silence had been increasing. Now he could contain his anxiety no longer. There had always been a weekly letter from her, unrevealing enough and stiff with the cautious, formal, outmoded phrases taken from the models provided by the popular letter-writers. And then, three weeks back, the letters had stopped. At first, Costa had soothed himself by the invention of reasonable solutions for this mystery. One letter — the first not to arrive — might have been lost in the post. People frequently complained that letters which they could prove to have been posted in Barcelona had never reached them. But then another week passed and this theory had to be dropped, and Costa decided that Elena must be ill. What else was there to imagine? Anything else was unimaginable. A third week came and went with Costa spending his evenings in the creation of imploring notes to be dropped ineffectively through the post-box into this inscrutable but terrifying silence. And now for the first time Costa realized fully what he might be losing. Now, as the empty days came and went, he knew that much as he had learned to endure a life that contained nothing but hope, he could no longer go on living with that hope removed. Elena absent, Elena slipping away from him, became unbearably beautiful. He took to staring for minutes at a time at the creased, hardly recognizable snapshot of her which she had given him when they parted.

The bus left at six in the morning. Costa dressed and went out quietly to avoid wakening Molina, who slept in the room above. It cost thirty pesetas to travel to Barcelona riding inside the bus, or twenty pesetas on the top. Costa could not afford comfort. He crouched uneasily on the low bench, clinging to the outside rail as the bus lurched round the bends. He wanted to be in Barcelona. Now that he had committed himself to action, the suspense had become unbearable.

Costa's companions on the bus-top were unhappy-looking peasants and fishermen, forced by matters of urgency into making this journey. The village people had a sour mistrust of the big city and all that it stood for. The vicious influence it generated was so real to them that, like the effluvium from a sulphur spring, its intensity increased or diminished in regular relationship to one's distance from it. Thus at Blanes, forty miles away, the urban infection was so slight that it only showed itself in certain meannesses of spirit. Fifteen miles farther along the road at Mataró, people already spoke with a city accent, and took advantage of strangers. While at Badalona, where the tramcars started zigzagging about the road, visiting rustics, struggling with their travel sickness, aroused themselves enough to make sure that the packets of money sewn into their coat-linings were still there.

The bus thundered on over the terrible road, shaken by the bumps and by the inner palsy of ruined gears and bearings, its passengers sun-roasted, dust-whitened, buffeted and sick. Finally even Costa's preying anxieties were overcome by his physical plight, and by the time they pulled up at their destination he was so weak that he could hardly climb down.

They had stopped by some gardens in an enormous square which was closed in by buildings like cliffs, and Costa, fatigue-drugged, saw a yellow trickle of taxi-cabs coming down cañons of white marble, tramcars showering blue sparks upon the heads of unprotesting pedestrians, and a sky full of pigeons and flags. He wanted to search out a quiet corner among the bushes, out of reach of the feet of these scurrying, absent-faced multitudes, where he might be allowed to stretch himself out a little, but a neat young man who made him feel dirty and stupid came up and put a fountain-pen into his hand, while another tried to fasten a watch on his wrist. With some difficulty and many apologies, he was able to excuse himself. And then, remembering the paper with Elena's address, he went back and showed it to the bus driver, who pointed to one of the streets leading out of the square. 'You'll find the turning about ten minutes walk up there, on the right. After that, it's the third or the fourth — I forget which — on the left. And don't forget to be here by nine if you want to get back tonight.'

Once he had escaped the young men with the fountain-pens and watches, nobody else in these hastening crowds showed the slightest interest in Costa. Suddenly he was isolated, forgotten in the city's sincere indifference, and when a policeman shouted at him as he followed a group of well-dressed citizens into the road at a pedestrian crossing without noticing that the electric sign had changed to 'halt' he felt almost relieved.

He had imagined that Elena would be working in a house like one of the black-marketeers' villas at Torre del Mar, with a garden and a discreet side entrance giving anyone the chance to approach and to tap on the kitchen window unobserved by the ladies and gentlemen of the house.

This address, when finally found, was quite different. It was in a quiet, tree-shaded street with big cars stealing by with a faint lick of tyres on hot asphalt, and notices prohibiting street noises of any kind. There undoubtedly was the number given on the paper, repeated on each side of a name scrawled illegibly in luminous tubing. The building was made of opaque glass blocks. Only the door was transparent, with a huge knob sprouting from the glass like a fungus of metal. Costa walked up and down for ten minutes and was about to ring the night bell, which was the only bell he could find when a car pulled up and a young lady got out. She crossed the pavement taking very quick, short steps. She had purple lips and an amazingly long neck. Perched on her fair, up-swept hair was what looked like a small pocket-handkerchief with a knot in one corner. From the aquarium depths of the room behind the glass a man dressed in some kind of naval uniform suddenly loomed up to open the door.

Costa tapped on the glass but was unable to attract the naval officer's attention. He waited a few minutes and then, very carefully, to avoid doing any damage, pushed open the door and walked nervously through it. For a moment he was like a skater on ice for the first time, as his feet slipped on the polished boards, flinging out his arms to recover his balance. Then treading cautiously, placing each foot squarely on the glistening surface and walking flat-footed, he reached the man in the dark blue uniform. 'Excuse me, sir. Sorry to put you to any bother. I wonder if you could inform me if a lady by the name of Nobell lives here?' Costa's voice sounded unpleasantly loud to him in the stillness of this polished chamber.

The distinguished man gave no signs of having heard. Not a muscle of his handsome face moved and his eyes were fixed on a point somewhere over Costa's right shoulder. Costa was about to repeat his question, phrased in a more respectful way, when the man bounded past him again to swing open the door for a lady who might have been the twin sister of the one who had previously entered.

The man came back, seeming now to notice Costa for the first time.

'Domestic?'

'I beg your pardon, sir?'

'A menial, a slavey?'

Costa shook his head. 'A young lady from Torre del Mar, helping out with a family called Porta.'

'Third floor, door on the right. Use the service lift.' He signalled to a buttons in the background.

The buttons, wondering and sympathetic, took him up, showed him the door and pressed a wall-button. Bells chimed sweetly in a remote interior; a pause, a distant voice said: 'I'm going, I'm going,' then the door opened releasing still, slightly perfumed air, and revealing a uniformed maid who looked annoyed with what she saw.

'Yes?'

'Please do me the favour . . . does the Señorita Nobell live here?'

'Wait a minute,' said the maid, closing the door.

There was a long wait, and then the door swung open silently again and she was there. He was shocked. After the glamour of the image that had been obsessing him, she was hardly recognizable. In a fraction of a second he took in the pale sallow face, the mouth bloodless and not clearly defined, the dull untidiness of the hair, the frightened, tremendous eyes. Then his emotions burst their bounds. He felt his eyes fill with water, and his mouth, opened wordlessly, begin to waver. She looked thinner, like a sister ten years older than herself, as she stood there in the stale, perfumed atmosphere, that smelt like a foreign woman. She was surprised, confused even; but whether she was pleased to see him or not, Costa couldn't tell.

Lamely she said something in the way of a greeting and held out a hand, which she had dried quickly on a dirty apron. 'You see, they don't allow friends to call at the house,' he heard her say. There was a cushioned rumble as the lift gates opened. She looked alarmed and drew him into the doorway. Behind her, he saw an astonishing painting on the wall of a pinkly nude woman looking out of a window. He was horrified that she should be exposed to such sights.

'Look,' she said, 'I'll try to get away in the afternoon for an hour, while they're having their siesta.' She pushed him towards the stairs. 'Wait for me down in the street at three. Whatever happens, I'll come down for a minute.'

He had walked about the neighbouring streets, taking care not to get too far away, deciding to be back there well before time, because after all there was always a chance that she might be free a little earlier than she expected. He waited, drifting between the trees from shade to shade, eyes mesmerized by the blind glass façade, while the street went dead in the afternoon's hush. He counted minutes that were less than half-minutes. The sun impaled itself on, then dropped divided behind a high spire. The first cruising taxis appeared. Before the next taxi passes, he said to himself . . . Well, then, before the next one. And in the end she did come, a flutter of white movement, moth-like behind the glass door, and then she was in the street, running towards him, waving gaily, self-composed, young again. 'Poor thing, how I made you wait! I thought I was never going to get finished.'

He was just going to ask if she was free for the rest of the evening when she said: 'I've only got an hour. Let's go and sit down in the gardens.'

Costa's doubts were settled. There was a change. Something was wrong between them. She had fortified herself with cosmetics and a newly pressed frock. After excusing the lapse in her correspondence — 'Really, I've been feeling so washed out. You know, when you only get an evening a week off, and what with headaches' — she kept him at arm's length with a quick, trivial monologue, full of city words and phrases. In the old days she would have been full of affectionate contempt. 'Really though, I ask you. What a sight you are! Like a principal mourner all dolled up to hear the will read.' Now it was, did he have a comfortable trip? And how was his mother's chest? The best thing for her would be to come to Barcelona, where the air was drier, although some people found the traffic kept them awake at nights. As for her, she could sleep through an earthquake. Her eyes rarely met his, but when they did she smiled quickly, and this too was not as it should have been. Politeness had slipped between them like a separating wedge.

Costa knew that only a physical contact could break this spell, close the sudden gulf that had opened between them. He longed for a secluded place where he could take both her hands and then talk to her, pressing them between his. He wanted to take her in the wordless embrace with which lovers believe they silence even the most fundamental disharmonies of their souls. But in all its splendour, with all the cunning insight with which Barcelona had been built for the furtherance of human pleasure and satisfaction, it lacked these simple essentials: the sheltering arches of a broken bridge, the angle of a derelict wall, the refuge of a clump of feathered bamboo. Here all space had been accounted for and there was no refuge from the gazing of incurious eyes and the absent eavesdropping of the world through a thousand windows.

'How far away are the gardens?' he asked, the gracious word bringing its associations of leaf-splashing fountains, remote from this echo-shouting back-drop of buildings, shimmering in their own heat.

'We're nearly there,' she said, increasing the pace. A

pause. 'I must be back by six.' She stopped to admire some article in a shop window, going into the recessed doorway to study it from another angle, and he felt hurt that she should be ready to squander their precious seconds in this way.

They turned corners, walked on, and turned more corners. Costa's feet, leather-encased for the first time for a year, were tiring. 'We're practically there,' she said. 'It's nicer to sit in the shade than to have to walk about the hot streets.'

But the gardens, when they reached them, were full of people who had gone to stroll there after awaking from their siestas. They sat on the end of a bench where two soldiers were already sitting, and a child with a hoop planted himself in front of them, staring.

'It's prettier here, isn't it?' she said.

'Yes.'

'Prettier than the Plaza de Cataluña, but not so pretty as the Plaza Real, but that's too far away. Do you know what I like about the Plaza Real? It's not as if it's a big square or anything like that — it's the fountain with all that moss on the top, and the pigeons, and of course those funny lamps. You should see the Plaza Real. There's a shop in the corner that sells stuffed things, birds and cats and crocodiles and things. If we had another ten minutes we could go down there by tram. We come here on our evenings off, sometimes. It's not worth going far when you have to go back so early. It's a nice square, isn't it? I love the flowers.'

'There's not much shade,' he said. The child who had wandered off was back again, impervious to Costa's glare.

A third soldier had arrived, and horseplay started between them.

'It's better later on,' she said, 'when the sun goes down a bit more. The lights shining through the leaves look very pretty.'

'Yes,' he said. 'I suppose it would be better then.'

He was longing for her and time was flowing away from them, but nothing would come but this foolish babble. The more he struggled to break into some speech which would convince her of his passion, the more stubbornly the words resisted him.

'Look,' she said, 'the roses are out already. Do you like roses?'

He nodded, feeling agonizingly the passage of the minutes. 'Doesn't it fly?' she said. He followed her gaze up to a huge clock advertising insurance, and as he looked the big hand jerked forward three inches.

'I'll have to think about moving in a few minutes.'

And then, he thought, they would walk back quickly through the now overflowing streets; they would have said nothing, the barrier between them would remain intact, he would lose her.

Sadly she said: 'I'd have liked a home with flowers trailing over the wall, not roses . . . What do you call those blue flowers?' She looked at him as if this question were one of real importance, her eyes meeting his for the first time without the smile of defence. 'The flowers hang down in bunches,' she said. 'I had the name on the tip of my tongue.'

Her tone had suddenly softened, and in his stumbling way Costa understood that in thus talking of a home of her own she had given him a last chance. And after this revealing sentence she had turned away quickly, but not in time to conceal from him the moisture which she had gathered on the back of a finger before it could become a tear. Hungrily, he seized her hand, and she only removed it to open the stiff, shiny handbag for her handkerchief and dab at her eyes with frank resignation to this escape of her emotions. 'There it is, you see,' all pretence surrendered now. 'Now I'd better go, before I make a spectacle of myself.'

'Stay another five minutes,' he said. 'Please don't go. I've something important to tell you.'

'What's the use?' she said. 'There's nothing much to be done now. It's a bit too late. I'm sorry for the exhibition.'

Costa forced her back into the seat, forced himself into the decision he had put off so long. 'Look, I wanted to tell you. I'm taking the old man's gear and starting up in Puerto de La Selva. We can get married, any time you want to. That's if you haven't changed about things.'

She looked almost angry, eyes dark and wide in the waxen face, with the colour painted incautiously over its pallor. 'Why couldn't you think of that before? You talk about changing about things!'

'Come on,' he said, 'pack up now and let's go away. After all what's to stop us?' It seemed to Costa that they had been imprisoned in a nightmare of his own invention, and that it had required only an effort of the will, or perhaps some final shock like this, to release them. Now he was awake at last. All they had to do was to take the nine o'clock bus together to freedom and happiness. His sense of responsibility to his mother was unmasked as some stupid subterfuge invented by something within him which he did not understand. Perhaps he had not really loved Elena until now. 'I'm not going to leave you here any longer,' he said. 'We'll go back together tonight. We've every right to lead our own lives.'

But she was shaking her head. 'How can I? You can't do that kind of thing. You can't just walk out of a job without giving notice. I mean there's the contract to be considered. It's no use being unreasonable . . . Oh, my God, just look at the time.' She jumped to her feet and pulled him after her. 'They don't even know I'm out. If only you'd have warned me, I could have asked to change my evening off.'

She scurried along, the high heels of her glossy shoes tapping impatiently on the pavement. 'Well, what are we going to do?' he said. 'If you want to go away, what's to stop you? They can't keep you here against your will.'

'I don't know,' she said. 'I suppose this has come as a bit of a surprise. It's a question of what's the best thing. I ought to have a day or two to think about it.'

'Look here,' she said a moment later. 'I'll think of something by tonight, and I'll write to you.' She brightened at the idea. 'Yes, I'll write before going to bed.'

'You won't write,' he said. 'You'll put it off, and I'll be waiting weeks again for a letter.'

'I'll write tonight,' she said. 'That's a promise.' Her voice faltered. 'Don't think I don't want to get away from this place. If only you knew!'

'Why ever did you leave home?' he asked. 'I don't know why you wanted to leave home?'

'I don't know, either,' she said. She was really crying

now, and the small, overpainted, anxious face had gone heartrendingly ugly, like that of a frightened child. The impulse to take her in his arms had never been so great, but the crowds kept them apart. There were crowds everywhere.

CHAPTER 12

THE first caller at the police-station that morning was Paquita, a gypsy who had spent the previous night with Don Federico Vilanova. Paquita did not know how old she was, giving her age variously, dependent upon her mood, at anything between twenty and twenty-five. Her beauty was of an uncommon type, vigorous and alien, the profile on an ancient coin or fragment of Carthaginian pottery, and its appeal was strong to those older men whose standards had been influenced by a classical education. Paquita startled most of the villagers with the flamboyance of her manner and her attire; the low-cut blouse and the defiant skirt stretched tight over hips that were big for a gypsy's.

Calles kept Paquita waiting half an hour, and when at last she was admitted she showed her bad temper by slamming the door. She then sat down, crossed her legs with an aggressive flash of brown thigh, felt in her blouse for a packet of cigarettes, and lit up.

'If you don't mind,' Calles said, 'no smoking here.'

Paquita clicked her tongue and threw the cigarette out of the window. 'I don't particularly enjoy hanging about out there, with that half-baked clerk, or whatever he is, staring at me.'

'As it happens, you've called at an inconvenient time,' Calles said. He sat at his writing-table with a half-written report in front of him, and had not put down his pen.

The visits of Paquita made him uneasy. 'Do you mind making it as brief as possible. And please pull your skirts down.'

'Where I come from they at least know how to treat you politely,' she said. She sniffed at the disinfectant in the air. 'This place stinks like a V.D. clinic.'

'Let's get down to business. What do you want?'

'I've got some more dope on Vilanova.'

The expression emptied out of Calles's face like a moneylender's who has smelt an unsound proposition in the offing.

'You don't seem very interested.'

'I'm not,' Calles said. 'We know all we want to know about him. He isn't really of the slightest importance.'

'So I've been wasting my time?'

'I don't know,' Calles said. 'Have you? Perhaps you have. You should know best.'

'Do you call that fair? I've worked hard on Vilanova, and now you turn round and say you aren't interested.'

'If you're still working on Vilanova, as you put it, it's for what you're getting out of it yourself. Don't expect me to believe anything else.'

'For what I'm getting out of it! Just listen to that! Why, you know as well as I do the old turkey cock hasn't got a couple of duros to rub together.' Paquita's lip curled towards a flaring nostril.

Calles shrugged his shoulders. He would have avoided this interview if he could, but now in some curious way he seemed to have resigned himself to it. He had become so used to the smell of Zotal that it no longer protected him from the strong, warm odour of Paquita's body.

'Look here,' she said, 'What's going to happen about Pépé?'

'For the moment, nothing,' Calles said.

'Are you going to sit there and tell me you're breaking your promise after all? I thought you said the case was coming up for review?'

'I made no promise whatever,' Calles said. 'It all depended on you. I made that clear enough, and as far as I can see you aren't making much of an effort to carry out your side of the contract.'

'Can you tell me what more I could have done? I must say you sang a different tune after you made me do the dirty on Torres.'

'You've been taking it easy since then,' he said. 'That was the only thing you did that was any help to us. For instance, they landed a million cigarettes not a couple of miles from here the other day. Everybody in the village knew about it, except you and your pals at the theatre, apparently.' Calles found himself looking for an excuse to humiliate Paquita. He was angry, and for some reason he did not want the feeling to pass. He did not know why he should feel as he did, but every time Paquita flaunted before him the scandalous details of her existence he had this sensation of anger and vindictiveness, as if in some way her behaviour involved his personal honour. Defensively, he reminded himself that nearly all police successes depended upon the goodwill of such informers. Paquita saw that he was watching her again. She shifted her position. The skirt slipped back above her knee. This time Calles did not look away. Abruptly, he said: 'It won't be convenient for you to come here again. People will get suspicious. I'll give you a private address.' There was a nervous stammer in the last sentence.

He wrote on a piece of paper, and Paquita, watching him, felt a thrill of triumph. All the fuss and bother, the begging and praying, and the dirty jobs — and in the end he had fallen, like anyone else, for a dose of the usual medicine! The old thigh-game. The three inches of smooth skin. The lion-tamer. Paquita knew that look only too well. She had caught him, eyes where they shouldn't have been, inspecting her like a bird tempted by the seed in a trap. All right, my fine feathered bird, you'll get your seed, next time. And you'll pay for it. She knew that type. Leave him alone with his imagination for a night or two. A private address — eh? If he could hold out for more than a couple of days, it would surprise her. And then, when the summons came, that would be the end of all her troubles, and the prison gates would open at last for Pépé.

With swinging hips she flaunted down the stairs, past the orderly room and out into the street, her black and scarlet focusing the sun's morning blaze. She heard the thin, debased wavering of oriental music from the tented theatre on the beach, where they were already rehearsing, and, loathing it all, she stopped and went into the Twentieth Century.

The Twentieth Century had been so named because it had been built in the year 1900, and its title was profoundly misleading. The café was a relic of the days when small fortunes were made locally from the cork industry. It had hot, black leather upholstery, looking like thick paper in the places where it had torn, a counter banked with obsolete paraphernalia of tarnished silver, an oleograph of the Eiffel Tower, and a morose old waiter with ulcers, who had worked there as a boy.

Paquita settled herself in a corner. At that moment there were six customers, sitting with empty glasses before them, all old men with stiff, black hats, winged collars and black ribbon bows. These were the owners of the cork forest who had been more or less ruined by the invention of the metal bottle-top, and now they had much leisure in which to keep up appearances. They all shaved every second day, the skin at the corners of their tightly compressed mouths looked as if it had been gripped up by invisible pegs, and anyone coming close enough to them could never make out whether the smell of leather existed in reality or only in the imagination. They weighed her up with their old, shrewd, tolerant, complacent, disillusioned eyes, heads thrust out, turtle-like, as if from armoured shells under which they could retire at the slightest alarm.

A countryman drifted through the door, carrying with him a reek of byres, a little hard laughter and defeated purpose, and feeling the coins in his pocket. He caught her eye, gave his duros a last derisive jingle, turned and went out. A few fishermen came in and settled down to drink wine out of a porrón. They were laughing, boastful fellows, but easily scared off, and therefore no good to Paquita either. Half an hour passed, and the only fresh arrival was a man selling newspapers who half camouflaged his occupation by only carrying one newspaper at a time, as if he had bought it to read himself.

What a collection of skinflints! If only she could get away from all this miserliness and misery, and go back home where, however poor they were, they at least knew how to live. If only that fool of a Pépé hadn't got himself thrown into gaol. Well, say what you like, there was a man if ever there was one. All she asked of a man was that he should be a man, which none of her casual lovers ever were. And when Paquita thought of a man, she had in mind a splendid composite of all the vices that attracted her. He must be aloof, know how to stimulate her worship with indifference and undependability, a spendthrift — with her money if necessary — rewarding her for her subservience occasionally with a few words of flattery; recklessness she adored, and did not object to the vain-glory that went with it, or to a cold heart and a store of lies. Above all she wanted to be allowed to love without return. Never to be loved, or pursued. And the only man she had ever known who conformed to such an ideal was Pépé, who now lay in gaol. Calles was her only hope and, pining for the exalted misery of her former existence with Pépé, she longed for Calles to be a normal man, vulnerable in the way of any ordinary male. She supposed there was something wrong with the way he was made; a queer of some kind, who probably slept with his driver batman.

She looked up, hearing the door open and close. Another customer had come in. A foreigner, she thought, by his clothing, and a bit dried-up looking, but at least a possibility. Perhaps in response to the interest of her glance, he threaded his way through the tables towards her and seated himself at the next table. When, from the corner of her eye, she knew that he was studying her profile, she turned her head suddenly and gave him one of those wide-open, cards-on-the-table smiles of hers that did the trick more often than not. 'Look here,' she said, 'I'm going off my head for someone to talk to in this place. Let's have a drink together.'

Molina got up and came and sat down at the table beside her.

CHAPTER 13

MOLINA slept little and late, and even then with many interruptions. A ship's siren at sea with its sweet, brief, booming echo disturbed him; he was awakened by the watchman who went the rounds calling the fishermen from their beds, and by the driver of the bus that took Costa to Barcelona racing his sluggish engine and crashing his gears.

When he awoke finally it was nearly ten by the clock on the church tower. A hot wind was coming from the south, breathing rather than blowing, and the mountains had gone back a little. Molina dressed and went up on to the roof, which was enclosed by a low, ornamental stone parapet. Here a small, windowless, brick building had been built, occupying about a third of the space. Narrow iron posts had been fixed in the four angles of the parapet and wires had been strung between them which had been used in the past by the old mother to dry her washing.

This house was built on a gentle slope on the town's outskirts and, although Molina could overlook the roof-tops of the neighbouring fishermen's houses, he himself was free from observation except from the villas of the rich, built on the hillside behind, the nearest being a good hundred yards away. He surveyed the street below, for the moment possessed only by foraging cats, crouched at all the angles, bellies pressed into the dust, noses testing the air. Light was tossed from white wall to white wall, and all the windows looking to the south had gone blind with sun. A casement opened silently and a woman, ripping the intestines out of a fish, dropped them into the street; the cats streaked inwards. A party of foreigners dressed in the strange uniforms of pleasure broke from the shadows into the light. There were many foreigners in Torre del Mar now. Their keen faces, a curious mixture of happiness and suspicion, demanded as they searched for Spain's eternal but elusive carnival, 'Ou c'est la fête?' Thin, squeaking music from portable wireless sets reached Molina's ears from the four quarters of space. The more foreigners the better, he thought.

He stepped back from the parapet, immediately cutting off his view of the town with the exception of a row of chimney pots with their archaic, Moorish-looking wind covers. He went into the small windowless building. It proved to be a store for fishing gear. Here were stored, each in its place, the dark brown nets, the lines, the tridents of different lengths, the circular lead-weighted nets called raïs, the obsolete acetylene lamps used in the past on the sardine boats, the elaborate fishpots of varying sizes, shapes and purposes. Here the orderliness of a Catalonian home had become static and sacrosanct since the father's death. A little white powder stood on everything.

Molina went down into his room and came up with the case containing the transmitter, which he had finished constructing the day before, and a coil of insulated wire. He lifted the heavy corner of a sail, dislodging a small shower of dust, pushed the case underneath and let the thick canvas drop back. When he took the end of the clothes-line between his thumb and finger, it crumbled.

Unrolling the coil of wire, he measured the approximate length, cut it off and stretched it from pole to pole across the roof in place of the clothes-line. The clean, white cotton covering of the insulated wire looked startlingly new against the blue of the sky. For the first time since he had crossed the frontier Molina was beginning to feel confident. That night, or the next night, he would establish contact with his headquarters and transmit the information about the time and place for the landing that would complete his mission. After that he would carry the transmitter in the darkness to the top of the nearest cliff, drop it into the sea, and take the first train back across the frontier. And then he would feel free to wash his hands of it all, to set up as a mechanic, perhaps, in some forgotten village down by the sea in the Camargue, where the days were changeless; perhaps in the end even find some neglected, dowry-less girl to marry him.

When Molina left the house that morning it was with the intention of walking a great deal. He would get the air into his lungs, uncover his skin to the sun, perhaps climb an easy cliff. Time was short and he felt the need to toughen his body, to ward off the physical decline that would end by betraying him. Molina feared that the courage of which he stood so much in need was linked too closely with nerve fibres, blood condition, bowel movements. The spirit kept pace with the body, flagged and went flabby with it, aged with it. In the end, cowardice lodged in the cells like a virus disease. The toughest man who ever lived would confess to crimes he had not committed if deprived of sleep for a week.

For a brisk hour he walked. Then suddenly he felt tired and bored, and finding himself, not entirely without design, outside the café where he had met the gypsy, went in.

The Twentieth Century was full of fishermen, noisily good-humoured after the night's work. He ordered a quarter of a litre of red wine. A young fisherman sat at the table, very handsome, nose peeling, left hand bandaged where the nylon line had cut him. He grinned at Molina, on good terms with the world. 'Foreigner, eh?'

Molina said, 'French.'

'French,' said the young man, nodding, 'and very nice too. Been to Marseilles myself. They know how to rook you there all right . . . But apart from that . . . Speak Spanish pretty well, don't you?'

'I was born here,' Molina said.

'That's what I should have said. As soon as I heard you order a quarter of red, I said to myself, even if he never bought that suit in Spain, he speaks Spanish as well as I do. Well, so you're back again. Nothing like it, after all, is there?'

'No,' said Molina. 'Nothing like it.'

'Over there,' said the young man, 'you knock up the money and no mistake. But what have you got to show for it all? It goes just as quick as it does anywhere else, and no one to give you a civil word into the bargain. It takes a bit of seeing the world to show you where you're well off.'

Molina nodded. He had been used to argue that if men lived long enough under an odious tyranny they would finally adapt themselves just as well as Esquimaux did to the eternal snow or the Bedouin to his desert. And he would have explained that they had to be educated out of this terrible complacency, this foolish, craven endurance.

'So you prefer life here?'

'Who wouldn't, after all? It was a bit — you know what I mean — after the war, but that's a thing of the past now. They had to go out for the tourists, so there you are. I mean they can't afford to be any different in the way they treat people from any other country where the tourists go, otherwise they wouldn't get any tourists. Tourism, that's what they're after. That's all that matters these days.'

The treacherous pessimism that always lay in wait for him had seized its chance and was presenting its insidious arguments. Yes, Molina thought, this was the final answer. Where a generation of dedicated revolutionaries had failed, a few seasons of touristic invasions would succeed. Spain would be democratized, hurled forcibly into this century, not by the sacrifices of its exiled reformers, but by the need to put on a good face for the benefit of spenders of sought-after currencies. Molina had heard of a place near Huesca where they had civil guards permanently on duty to prevent foreigners photographing the troglodytes, and if they showed that they were ashamed in this way it was only a step to getting the people out of the caves and putting them into houses. Molina was unable to delude himself into a denial of his disappointment that change, even for the better, should come in this way, and then he realized that thoughts like this were leading to the shocking conclusion that the revolutionaries' motives might not be so pure as they themselves supposed. Could it even be that they wanted revolution not for Spain, but for their own ends? Molina tried to stop thinking, to summon the unreasoning wordless voice that in the past had come to his rescue, that arrogant conviction that once had annihilated doubts as soon as born, but which now had deserted him.

'To tell you the truth,' the fisherman said, 'if there's one thing we're badly off for here, it's education. Look here, don't go on drinking that stuff. Have a brandy with me. You know, the kids only put in a couple of hours a day, with one master between sixty or seventy of them, all ages too, so what can you expect? I suppose you speak English as well as French. That's wonderful. If I could speak foreign lingoes like that I wouldn't want to call the king my cousin.'

Molina felt rebuked in his defeatism. Here the first young man he'd struck up conversation with was admitting his thirst for knowledge. He was ashamed of that sly, lurking cynicism that had sprung at him with so little provocation.

'You ought to get together and start classes among yourselves,' he said. 'Surely someone could give you a hand. I wish I were staying long enough myself.'

The fisherman had been fumbling in his pocket and now he drew out a piece of crumpled, rather dirty paper, smoothed it with the palm of his hand on the table, and handed it to Molina. 'I'm doing my best to pick up a few words here and there, as I go along. It's slow going, you know. Wonder if I could trespass on your kindness to ask you to write down what it says there in English?'

Molina took the paper on which had been printed, in

awkward schoolboy characters, several words and phrases in Spanish. He read:

You are very beautiful. Please dance with me.

A sailor's life is beset with danger.

A little sympathy.

To kiss.

To embrace.

To have intercourse with.

I must go. Perhaps we shall meet again.

The young man smiled charmingly. 'Many English ladies come to stay at the new hotel.'

Molina wrote down the required translation and the young man thanked him effusively and left soon after, to put into service, Molina supposed, his newly acquired knowledge. He couldn't help laughing to himself. If you're prepared to let that kind of meeting influence you one way or another there isn't really much hope for you.

A few minutes later the gypsy came in, hovering for a moment like a butterfly, impaled in space by the grudging lust of the men's glances, then, seemingly without even looking in Molina's direction, making straight for his table. She fell into a chair, took his arm by the wrist and shook it. She had untidy, bluish-black hair — too much of it, Molina thought — and the strength and attraction of her face were concentrated at a point somewhere between the eyes, which were strangely shaped. Molina found that her tiny, white, sharp-pointed fingers reminded him of the neat front paws of some burrowing animal. She caught his glance at the man's wrist-watch which she was wearing, with its cheaply modernistic face. 'My boy-friend's,' she said. 'He's doing time. The last thing between me and the doghouse. Do you know how much they wanted to give me on it? Twenty pesetas.'

Molina studied the wonderful unfamiliarity of her features. Certainly not a postmistress in the Camargue by any stretch of the imagination. Yet extremes might easily meet and join hands when it came to such a matter as turning one's back on the world. 'How's the theatre doing?' he said.

She put her hand to her face as if afraid that the violence of her disgust might throw it into some permanent dislocation. 'Need you ask? Those swine. We put on a cuadro flamenco and they don't like it. We even learn to dance sardañas, but no, that's no good either. Anywhere north of Valencia it's like that. They want to see performing seals. Down south we used to play to full houses every night. I could show you the cuttings.'

'Why didn't you stay where you were well off?'

She had no ready-made answer for this question. She had never even considered it. One moved on because one did. Molina watched her puzzled expression, thinking: We're all like parasites coughed out of a pig's lung, driven on by something we've no control over, through intestines and excrement towards an end we haven't the faintest idea of. What strange lemming impulse, for example, had driven these flamenco dancers out into such chilling wastes?

'But then, after all, what's to stop you going back, or moving on?'

'I told you,' she said. 'Or perhaps I didn't. The boy friend. He's the one who looks after the lorry. The engine's in bits. Added to which we can't even raise the wind to buy petrol. So you might say we're stuck here until further notice.'

The old waiter was there facing them, dry-coughing, impatient.

'What's it to be?' Molina asked.

'Something that lasts. Half a minute though — you're paying, aren't you? I'll have a brandy.'

'Two Ricardos,' said the waiter, already moving away.

Paquita jumped up and pulled him back. 'Ricardos? — who said anything about Ricardos? I want a Jaime Primero.'

'We don't have it.'

'A Pedro Domecq then.'

'Only inferior brands in stock,' the waiter said. 'If you want anything fancy you'll have to go somewhere else.'

'Did you hear that?' she said. 'Only inferior brands! Well, for the moment I've had enough of inferiority, so I'll go without.'

The waiter went off, grumbling aloud. The poorer they were the more airs they gave themselves. If I'd have said nothing, given her a Ricardo and charged her for a Jaime Primero, she wouldn't have known the difference. But then he knew she was quite capable of asking to see the bottle. Why didn't all those beggars stay and starve in Andalusia, where they belonged?

'I've got nowhere to sleep,' Paquita said suddenly. 'I don't say that because I want you to take pity on me. I state it as a fact you might be interested to hear.'

Molina studied her again, that face from the classical past, the velvet shadow projecting from the chin over the soft, wave-like gliding muscles of the throat, the cheap, shabby glamour of her dress.

'How does that happen?'

'The individual who's supposed to be manager feels drawn to me. He wears a tube in his stomach. I prefer to keep away from the place until he gets over it. At night, I mean.'

'And where *do* you go?'

'Wherever I can. Usually the beach. It wouldn't be so bad if it wasn't for the mosquitoes. Funny how soon anyone gets into bad habits. I was ten years old before I slept in a bed, and now I'm turning up my nose at good, clean sand and a few mosquitoes.'

Molina, watching her, disturbingly happy that she should be there, at grips with the untried, unmanageable happiness of the recluse, knew that the time had come when he should have found some excuse to get up and leave. There were a forthrightness and a kind of courage about the gypsy that awakened in him a dangerous sympathy, and Molina knew that security lay in refusing to see this girl as a human being but as a safely de-personalized symbol of suffering and degradation. One of the austere rules of his calling was this: never to divert one's strength into a wasteful solicitude for individuals, never to clothe the sufferings of the masses, kept at a distance, in flesh and blood. A year before, the very notion that this girl's fate could have had the slightest interest for him would have sent Molina into a hasty retreat behind his defences. But now the defence system was crumbling all along the line. 'Do you want to go and look for your drink somewhere else?' he asked her.

'There isn't anywhere else, and anyway, I don't want to drink any more. It's the thought of this afternoon that's getting on my nerves.'

'What happens this afternoon?'

'The show. The afternoon performance. If only you could see their faces, you'd know what I meant — when they don't understand what it's all about and they start laughing. Do you mind keeping talking, so that I can take my mind off it?'

'There's something I want to keep my mind off too,' Molina said. 'Let's go for a walk along the cliffs.'

CHAPTER 14

DON FEDERICO VILANOVA mounted his two-stroke motor cycle and, sitting up rather like a praying mantis to grasp the wide, upswung handlebars, went puttering slowly down the hill into the village. He visited the municipal offices, bought a quart of petrol at the grocer's, then yielded to the temptation to linger in a café. He slipped into the Twentieth Century, settled himself in his usual corner and, looking round, saw Dr. Rosas. Rosas was with a foreign couple with whom he had scraped an acquaintance. The woman had a great deal of very pale golden hair and an expression that appeared and vanished in the neat-featured face as if in response to electric signals. Rosas, who was an admirer and a connoisseur of coldness in women, was gazing enraptured into her eyes. Don Federico, feeling still aggrieved after their last meeting, looked away hastily, but Rosas had already seen him and, anxious to put things right again with the old man, came bouncing over to his table.

'Still at it, I see,' Vilanova said sourly.

'She's an American and she's wonderful,' Rosas said. 'So unhappy because she's just found out she's still in love with her first husband. I think I can be of help to her.'

'With vitamins, I suppose?' Vilanova asked.

'No, psychotherapy in this case.'

Vilanova tasted his coffee and let out a yelp of dissatisfaction. He put down the cup and looked at Rosas curiously. 'Didn't you lose a front tooth the last time you took a psychotherapeutic interest in someone else's wife?'

Rosas grinned at him. 'No, I shook that out in a fit of neurotic coughing.'

Don Federico studied the doctor's face with distaste, the pink cheeks, small blue eyes, knowing grin. Hide like a rhinoceros, he thought. Rosas had put a book down on the table. Its lurid dust jacket promised rape and murder, and a band of scarlet paper worn round its middle bore the claim that over a million copies had been sold in Europe alone.

'What's that you're reading?'

'A lively piece of pornography from Italy, about the antics of the Anglo-Saxons in Naples. It's in enormous demand. Hard work to chisel it out of the people at the bookshop. Do you want to borrow it?'

'No, thanks,' said Vilanova, making a face. 'I'll stick to my banned classics. I'm re-reading Montaigne at the moment.'

Rosas opened the book, glanced at a page, and closed it, chuckling. 'What wonderful people they are. The Americans, I mean. Just like you see them on the films. Do you know, there were a couple of girls who went out just before you came in, who give cigarette lighters away to any of our young fellows who feel like taking them out for a bit of fun. The village's glutted with them. Just imagine it, a woman given away with a cigarette lighter in a place like this where you expect to have to save up for ten years for one.'

Don Federico saw an opportunity for mounting his hobby horse. 'Before we go any further, can you tell me how many couples there are in this village who've been waiting up to ten years to get married and can't?'

'About twenty, I should say.'

'And why can't they marry?'

'Because they're hard up.'

'Or rather because all the houses put up here are sold at impossible prices to black-marketeers from the city. Am I right?'

'Absolutely.'

'So numerous human beings, who otherwise would have been brought into the world, aren't?'

'Right again, but where is all this leading to? Am I supposed to find something intolerably wrong in the way things are?'

'Well, don't you?'

'No,' said the doctor. 'I don't. I could tell you a lot of things that worry me more.'

'You're a poor kind of man,' Vilanova said, 'the kind that never looks beyond his personal satisfactions. It would be a bad outlook for the human species if we were all like you.'

'Or like you,' Rosas said, 'malcontents who take care to keep their grousing for the benefit of reliable friends. Look here, Don Federico, it's time we understood each other. I don't agree with you, and let's leave it at that. It's my belief that we weren't intended to have all our problems solved for us. It's still the survival of the fittest here, and I believe that's a good thing.'

They were interrupted by the entry of a group of fishermen, swept through the door, as if by a following wind. The men were noisily cheerful from a morning's good fishing, re-arranging chairs and table with a great deal of scraping and scuffling before they settled down. One of them moved across the café to cut off the old waiter before he could retire behind his screen of urns. 'Come here, Jaime. We want you. Where are you off to? Here, catch hold of him someone before he locks himself in the W.C.'

'Some fresh wine in a clean porrón, and within the next half-hour, Jaime, if that's not asking the impossible.'

'I'm too busy to bother about you, get it yourself,' the waiter said. He added an unusually filthy old-fashioned oath, which produced a shout of delight from the men.

Rosas said, 'I have the acute love for Spain of a man who has seen something of the rest of the world. I believe we're the happiest and most fortunate people on earth.'

'You're mad,' Vilanova said.

'God has blessed us with poverty.'

'Vitamins first, and now cant.' Vilanova's eyes were turned ceilingwards in protest.

'And poverty begets virtue. Abstemiousness, fortitude, spirituality — they're the virtues of our people.'

'I notice you have the good sense not to include chastity.'

'As human beings we thrive on a certain amount of bad government. I wouldn't care for less than we get. In France they go in for rights, and in America liberty. Did you observe the man sitting with that beautiful girl I was talking to?'

Vilanova followed his glance.

'He tells me he's a professor of philosophy, and he's got

so much liberty he's practically drowning in it. I hear he's still drunk when he gets up in the morning. The waiter has to dress him.'

'And what is that supposed to prove?'

'He's the man of the future, the product of wealth, democracy and boredom. He'll die of a broken heart. There's nothing to keep him on his toes. He reminds me of one of those over-fed broken-hearted animals in the Zoo. Here life's still an adventure. Just listen to those fishermen talking. They're the product of the benighted past.'

'Be serious now,' Francisco was saying, 'and let me tell you how the morning went.' He placed a restraining hand on the arm of the man next to him. 'It was a splendid morning in the bay. Be quiet now while I tell you what a fishing you missed.'

Francisco fixed his eyes dramatically on an horizon that appeared suddenly, shining through the dingy café walls. His voice, a little hushed, seemed to carry more clearly than before.

'Luck ran with me — ' ('Listen,' said Rosas, 'listen').

' — At dawn I visited the tide and, seeing that the day bore no malice, took the boat and went into the deep sea, where the great waves moved — '

'As illiterate as a conquistador, or one of the Catholic Kings,' Rosas whispered. 'They talk like characters out of Lope de Vega, and they're the grandest people on earth. Do you mean to tell me that if they'd been born just across the frontier, could read the sporting papers, eat meat every day and had a pocketful of rights they'd be any better for it? — I say, where are you off to so suddenly?'

Vilanova, who had risen to his feet said: 'As you see, I've finished my coffee.'

'Oh, I beg your pardon. I didn't notice. And so naturally you clear off without further ado!'

'I'm sorry,' Don Federico said. 'You must admit I usually make an effort to bear with you, but today I've a preference for my own company. I've just had some news that makes me even less inclined than usual to listen to a display of mental shallowness.'

Rosas sat glaring at his back as he made for the door. The insolent old fool! This really is the end, so far as I'm concerned. He can chase after me until he's blue in the face. In fact, I'd far sooner stop coming to this place than risk running into him again.

'Give me my bill,' he said to the waiter, 'I don't like the class of customer who comes here.'

'*You* don't like them?' said the waiter. 'I wonder what you imagine I think of them!'

CHAPTER 15

AS soon as Don Federico left the café he felt sorry for his display of ill-humour. I must do something to take myself in hand before it's too late, or I won't have a friend left — not that that would matter much, he couldn't help adding. Perhaps there's a little more excuse for me this time, he thought. That morning he had received a letter from his son breaking the news that, as a result of an inquiry into a student demonstration which had taken place more than a year before, he had been sent down from the University. Can I have been to blame in any way? Don Federico was worrying. The timing of this blow might have possessed a significance, coming as it did immediately after the colonel's visit. Poor fellow. His career's done for. I deserve to have my tongue cut out if it's happened all through my stupid, blundering way of going on.

He pressed the bulb of his horn and turned into the main street; as he did so, an untidy-looking civil guard darted out and stopped him.

'Can you read?'

For a moment Vilanova was startled. 'I beg your pardon?'

'There's a notice up there. What does it say?'

Struggling to keep his temper, Don Federico looked up and read 'One-Way Street'.

'All right,' said the civil guard. 'Now go round by the other way. And try to keep awake next time.'

'Look here my good fellow . . .' Vilanova started to protest. He saw no reason why he should be deprived of the use of a perfectly empty street and was furious at the guard's insolent manner. But it was clear that the guard was quite ready to arrest him, so Vilanova was obliged to turn back after all and use the bad road along the sea front.

For the first few yards fury blinded his powers of observation, then suddenly he became aware of a remarkable change that had taken place since last he had passed this way some three months before. Previously the sea road had held a somnolent confusion of boats, a few figures moving silently among them, and black-hooded crones bent over their nets under the low waterfront of ramshackle sheds where the sardines had been salted. Now the road was a vacant, sterile sash marked off from the beach by small bay trees in coloured tubs. Where the malodorous sheds had been, arose palatial buildings, almost painful in their dazzling whiteness under the noon sun.

The founders of Torre del Mar had built with cautious practicality, employing the cheapest local material — which happened to be a good-looking sandstone — and keeping well in mind the situation's vulnerability to winter storms. They built wide, squat, strong houses with their backs to the sea, crouching for shelter behind each other like a planned defence system. It was a pure accident that the result was pleasing, and that a visual harmony had been distilled from the forethought of builders who had concerned themselves only with the gales and revolutions to come.

Now the black-marketeers had descended upon the village — men who were no more impressed by the sea and the winds than they were by the law — and a side of their characters which was impractical, idealistic, even visionary, found its expression in the construction of fantastic palaces in sites which were defiantly exposed to the elements. These were confected of Californian-Moorish architecture, with stained glass, electric carillons, chimney pots in imitation of gnarled tree trunks, crazy pavements, and rotating sprinklers bedewing the grass of unnatural lawns. And here, with good-natured cynicism, the disreputable princes of the black-market led their private lives, preyed upon by a horde of sponging relations and grudgingly admired by the villagers who were exploited by them quite indirectly, and only then at a distance.

Astounded by this almost heavenly vision, Vilanova slowed down. There was a party of some kind going on outside the first palace. A table had been put out in the roadway, and round this a number of persons were being served with champagne. Don Federico knew that such open-air entertainments were in accordance with the tastes of the black-marketeers, who liked to show themselves as much as possible. He recognized the man who would be the host, a certain Alfonso Valls, a suave, abstemious ruffian, who had reappeared in the village after an absence of several years. At that moment Valls was telling a funny story. He was surrounded by an inner ring of sycophants and an outer circle of old aunts in mourning and distant cousins, and whenever the great man laughed the sound was taken up by his close cronies and spread outwards, like a ripple on a pond, through relations of decreasing importance until the most aged and unimportant great-aunt raised her fan to screen a toothless cackle.

Vilanova had slowed to a walking pace, his machine puttering unsteadily. The party had left very little room to pass, and he was about to negotiate the rutted sand between the table and the road's edge when Valls suddenly caught sight of him and, pushing back his chair, jumped up and rushed out into his path. Vilanova turned his wheel sharply to avoid him, his engine stalled, and throwing out a leg to save himself he fell heavily against Valls, who caught him in his arms. Two guests, bleating anxiously, rushed to their aid and relieved Don Federico of his motor cycle.

'My dear Vilanova' — Valls paused to pant — 'I hope I didn't startle you. You're such an impossible man to contact. I couldn't let the opportunity pass.'

Don Federico removed the hand from his shoulder. 'A dangerous lunatic,' he said. Valls smiled appeasingly with gay, bulging eyes, showing five large, good, slightly yellowed teeth above and three below. He was a bulky, success-fattened man. There was a good-natured, vulgar magnetism about him that Vilanova detested, but as soon as the smile died away a kind of sad intellectuality of expression returned. 'How could I expect you to remember me, when you haven't seen me since I was a whipper-snapper? I'm Alfonso. Alfonso Valls. Does the name mean anything?'

'It does,' Don Federico said. 'I remember you very well. You were sent to a reformatory, weren't you?'

The frank smile came again, rueful now, accompanying a head-shake. All the guests, who had by this time retired to a respectful distance, seemed to smile ruefully too, as if in some way emotionally synchronized with their host.

'Better to be remembered even by that than forgotten altogether, I suppose,' Alfonso said.

'Would you be so good as to restore my motor cycle?'

'Look here,' Alfonso said, 'you really must forgive me for waylaying you like this, but what's one to do when you're not at home to callers and you don't answer letters? I've a very important question to discuss with you. I assure you it won't take a moment.' He hustled Don Federico to a table, the big body galvanized with quick, lizard movements. The guests, heads slightly inclined, twirled their champagne glasses silently in the background.

Don Federico found himself abstractedly contemplating a map spread out on the table in front of him.

'This will interest you,' Alfonso said breezily.

'I can't see why it should,' Vilanova said, 'not in the slightest.'

'I've just become a landowner,' Alfonso said. 'That accounts for the celebrations. All the land for several miles round here used to be owned by three men. Now it's owned by two. You and me. I just bought out the other pair.'

'I'm sincerely grieved to hear it.'

'Oh come now,' Alfonso said. 'That's hardly the way to congratulate a new neighbour. Aren't you prepared to drink a glass of champagne with me?'

'I don't care for champagne,' Don Federico said. 'If

you've gone in for landowning now, good luck to you. I'm still sorry to hear that the others should have felt obliged to sell out.'

'They jumped at the chance,' Alfonso said. Several fishermen went past in a quick, burdened trot, bowed a little under the weight of the nets which they had just taken to be dyed. The reddish-brown dye streamed like blood down forearms and shanks. One of them lifted a free hand, and Alfonso raised an empty champagne glass in their direction and said: 'Happy days.' He picked up the map, shook it like a rat and, dropping it back on the table, gave it an affectionate slap. 'I'm going to put some money in your pocket,' he said to Vilanova.

'What did you say?' Don Federico was startled. He caught himself glancing down as if to make sure his clothing had suffered no polluting contact. Alfonso's finger moved across the big-scale map, ripping through hillsides, plunging down valleys to the coast.

'Have you any idea at all how much land you've got?'

'What a monster!' Don Federico said, as if expressing this opinion to some invisible third person.

'I'm ready to wager you haven't the foggiest. The other two old fellows hadn't. Look, you go up to this ridge, follow the edge for two thousand metres, and then down this valley. You extend to the left bank of the stream.' Alfonso's diamond-ringed finger jogged about the map like a camel carrying a precious load. 'It's all the barest rock. Like the surface of the moon.'

'Really?'

'The most barren land between here and the Sahara. I only mention this in passing, because I'm going to take the bitters with the sweets. This so-called copse is yours. All the wood's been strangled out of it by the undergrowth. It will cost a good bit to clear it up.'

'More than it's worth, I expect.' Don Federico suddenly found himself pleased with the direction the conversation had taken.

Valls waved a deprecatory hand. 'The way I do business you don't just pick out the plums.' His finger moved on. 'Things brighten up a bit down here. You've got a patch of soil the size of a postage stamp that used to grow melons thirty years ago.'

'Vegetable marrows,' Vilanova said.

'. . . and on this slope I see there are a few vines.'

'Producing a small, bitter grape, the size of a pea,' Don Federico added.

'Well, I suppose one could always replant.'

'Not in that situation,' Don Federico said. 'The spring dried up years ago.'

'Lucky that doesn't affect the cork oaks up there,' Alfonso said. 'You've a couple of hundred fairish trees.'

'They've got the weevil in them. A new kind — I forget its name. You'll find they've spread to that big plantation you've just acquired lower down the valley. I hope some allowance was made in the purchase price.'

Alfonso laughed. 'I'll remember to go into that. Now what have we here? Ah yes — do you realize, for example, that you're the owner of a gold mine? So far as I know, it never threatened to put Peru out of business before it closed down in the seventeen-hundreds. And then, of course, there's this pretty beach of yours. Do you know what I see here? I see a really first-class hotel, with one of those places where foreigners go to bake their skins off — a Lido — isn't it?'

'I don't,' Vilanova said.

'You don't what?'

'See an hotel and a Lido.'

'I mean in the mind's eye. In the visionary sense,' Valls said in the voice he used when talking to children of ten or under.

'Not in any sense.'

'Your father,' Alfonso said, 'paid three centimos a palmo for that land. The current market price is thirty centimos. I'll pay you fifty. You notice that my way of doing business is straight and to the point. It saves unnecessary discussion. I never haggle.'

'Nor do I.'

'In that case . . .?'

'In that case, with your permission, I'll withdraw.'

'Then my proposition's of no interest?'

'None at all.'

Valls folded the map and put it in his pocket. He was of a philosophical temperament and never permitted his frame of mind to be disturbed by temporary reverses.

'I hope you won't be sorry.'

'Why should I?' Vilanova asked.

'I don't know. It's a good offer. People are sometimes sorry when they realize they've turned down a good offer. Things happen. Circumstances change.'

'Not in my case,' Vilanova said.

'Well, you never know. In any case, no harm done. You know where I live, if you want to change your mind.'

Don Federico mounted his motor cycle, kicked the

starter, wobbled a little as the machine moved forward and then, steadying himself, accelerated hard in the hope of raising a little dust.

Alfonso Valls watched him for a moment, then called his secretary over. 'I want to make a long distance call. It's a Madrid number.'

CHAPTER 16

ON the morning of his return from Barcelona, Costa was called to the barracks of the civil guard. What was extraordinary about the summons was the method of its delivery. He was on his way down to the creek, quivering internally in his impatience to get the boat out and row over to Moors-in-Hell to find out whether the big merou had taken his hook. He had already been held up an hour waiting for the first of the boats to come in, for mackerel fresh caught that morning to use as bait, when the corporal stopped him. And here came the strange part. The corporal actually spoke as if he were addressing an equal. 'If you could make it convenient some time when you happen to be passing. The lieutenant would like a word with you.'

The lieutenant! Costa, a little dazed, looked past the young, clean-collared face, under the black, shiny wings of the patent leather hat, to a bruise in the cleanness of the horizon. The morning was breathless. A little black smoke hung over the water where a trawler had passed. A few boats were fishing close in. The day's going rotten like a damaged fruit, he thought. Give it three or four hours at the most. Almost a risk to go out as it was. But the lieutenant. Who'd ever dream of keeping a lieutenant waiting?

Once again the mould-smelling trunk had to be pulled out from under the bed for his holiday suit. He shaved, put on a stiff, greenish-black hat, and went out. Now, looking up, he saw the ragged, cat-shapes of clouds already clawing at the sky from the mountain tops. That decided it. There would be no fishing after he got back from his interview. What on earth could the lieutenant, of all people, want with him? Even to have a corporal address him civilly was remarkable enough.

There was a second surprise. Going along the sea-front, one of the fishermen lounging against the low wall actually spoke to him.

'Well, what do you think of it?' He nodded in the direction of the sky's distant discoloration.

'Not much,' Costa said. Then, feeling that on such an occasion not merely a politeness so much as a special effort of prognostication was called for, he said: 'Look at those clouds up there. I'd give it a couple of hours at the most.'

'Going out this morning?' asked the man, looking questioningly at Costa's dark, stiff, holiday suit.

'Just at the moment, I wouldn't like to say,' Sebastian said. 'See how things go.' He nodded towards the sky and risked a smile of resignation and mutual understanding.

'Me too,' said the fisherman, with a knowing wag of the head. 'It doesn't take one of those south-easterlies long to come up. Might chance it this afternoon, all being well.'

'In that case, good luck.'

'And good luck to you,' said the man. 'That's what we all need.'

'Let's hope it comes to nothing,' Costa said.

'Let's hope so.'

But while they had been talking a white line had been drawn right across the horizon, pencilling off sea and sky, where the waves lifted by distant winds were driving landwards. Men began to move down the beach in twos and threes to set about hauling the boats higher up the beach. Costa stopped again to join a line of men who were struggling with one of the heavier boats. They all thanked him, almost with warmth, he felt. One of the men, called Marco, had flopped down on the sand exhausted, and Costa took his place on the rope. Marco had been mutilated in the civil war and was a liability charitably shared among the boats. When the boat was secure at the higher level he limped over to Costa. 'Well, we shouldn't have known what to do with ourselves if it had lasted much longer. The luck, I mean. Might even have made some money.' Shrapnel had torn off one of Marco's cheeks and his voice issued through the resulting hole as well as through his mouth. Costa listened carefully, grateful to have been able to understand the grunts and gurgles that made up the sentences. 'Think the wind will blow away the tunny?' he asked.

There was a whistle of derision from the hole in Marco's cheek. 'Of course it will. The tunny showed up, so now we're in for a good stiff blow. It follows naturally, doesn't it?' Listening to his grumbles, Costa felt hope for the first time for many years. There was a promise of sympathy and comradeship in shared grousing. It was smooth, empty, unrevealing, self-concealing politeness he had to fear.

The road with the police-barracks was empty, but he

was just turning into the gateway when two men came round the corner, and after hesitating he walked straight on. For some reason no more than half-formed in his mind, he preferred not to be seen entering the police-barracks. People were summoned there for all kinds of reasons, but he thought there was no particular point in going out of his way to publicize the visit. All three men grumbled soft, perfunctory greetings as they passed. Costa did not look up. He turned the corner, walked a hundred yards, stopped to glance at the window of the new watch-shop, and came back. He passed through the gateway of the police-barracks, and the private who had been sitting on the stool got up quickly and signalled to him to go to the orderly room. Here the corporal he had already seen sat at a table, before which stood two men, recognized by Costa, even from their rear view, as those he had just passed in the street. The corporal was glaring at them sternly, and when he spoke his voice was a contemptuous, parade-ground bark. Seeing Costa he picked up a telephone. There was a click and the squeak of a voice at the other end, and speaking in a low voice the corporal said: 'Someone to see you, sir.' One of the two men risked a glance sideways and back at Costa. The voice in the earphone squeaked again, and the corporal said: 'Very well, sir,' and to Costa: 'Go up to the first floor.'

He found a door in the corridor marked 'Officer Commanding', and had raised his hand to tap when it opened and a woman came out carrying a scrubbing-brush and a pail of water. Close behind her, picking his way across the wet floor, came the lieutenant. 'Ah, come in, Costa.'

He smiled rigidly, holding out a hand. There was a fleck of dried metal polish on his belt buckle. 'Sit down here. Cigarette?'

Costa found himself sitting on the edge of a settee covered with worn tapestry. The lieutenant had come out from behind his desk and drawn up a chair. A fly-paper turned curling in a shaft of sunlight above his head. Costa clutched awkwardly at the cigarettes which were tight in the freshly opened State-monopoly packet. In pulling one out, he dislodged another and it fell to the ground. He scrambled to pick it up. 'Don't bother, don't bother,' said the lieutenant, his hand again extended holding a flaming lighter.

Costa stooped forward uncertainly, the end of his cigarette shaking in and out of the thin wedge of flame.

'My friend,' said the lieutenant, 'we haven't met before, but I know a good deal about you. As a matter of fact, I have a report here. It says you're a good chap.'

Costa couldn't think of anything to say. He was bewildered. The smile of encouragement seemed out of place, as if it had been grafted on to the lieutenant's thin, humourless face.

'Reliable people are only too rare in these days,' the lieutenant said. 'Let's hear something of your army record. You distinguished yourself as a soldier in the National Movement, didn't you?'

Costa nodded doubtfully. 'That's correct, sir.' Beneath his astonishment he was a little chilled by the lieutenant's affability; chilled, yet already feeling the beginnings of a slight intoxication from the effect of the approval of which he had so long been starved.

'Weren't you, in fact, decorated?' the lieutenant asked.

'Yes sir, in hospital, after Teruel.'

'Teruel,' said the lieutenant, staring at him curiously. 'Do you mind telling me what unit you were in?'

'The Nineteenth Navarra.' Costa announced the name of this famous infantry regiment with that certain matter-of-factness of tone which often emphasizes a boast. After all, he had fought with them — whether under compulsion or not — and bled with them, and here at last for a few fugitive minutes he could bask in the good opinion of another man on the strength of it. 'We caught it on the ridge.'

'Wonderful,' said the lieutenant quietly. 'Really, it's the most remarkable coincidence. I happen to have been there, too.'

'You were there, too, sir? Well, just imagine that. If it's not a presumption, what were you in?'

'The machine guns. The Nineteenth was on our right. They knew how to hold on. It would have been curtains for us if they hadn't.'

'I can hear them popping away now, sir — those guns,' Costa said. 'They put a few of us — picked men you understand — out in front to knock the teeth out of the counter-attack. We were keeping our fingers crossed, I can tell you.'

'Good man,' said the lieutenant. 'I suppose that's where you were wounded.'

'Only two of us came through. Both a bit knocked about. We took a terrible pasting. What else could you expect?' After the years of denial Costa's yearning for approbation had strengthened to a raging thirst. Once again he was ready to commit the unforgivable imposture, the terrible folly, of taking to his own credit the sardonic manœuvrings of fate.

War. He hated war. In his sober moments war was an absurdity, a predicament from which anyone but a complete fool longed only to extricate himself. But now he was drunk with fair words and wanted nothing so much as to strike the postures of the old soldier, to revel in memories of the easy, shallow sufferings which old soldiers collect and display for each other's benefit.

A new expression had broken through the professional mask into which over the last five years the lieutenant's face had gradually hardened. Suddenly he felt an acute pang of loneliness, and having once admitted its existence knew that he would be free from its importunings again. Calles would not look for temperament, affinity, wealth or standing in a friend. It would be enough, as in this case, that they had shared the same mighty, consecrating experience. Fate had picked each of them up, and they had been put down together in the same place and on the same sombre day. Oblivious of each other's existence, they had stood together and held off the same cruel enemy. The lieutenant realized now that he was unable to use this man for his own ends.

'How long have you been stranded in this place?' When the lieutenant said 'this place' he contrived to pour into the words a little of the disdain he felt for the empty godlessness of the Mediterranean shores.

'All my life, sir,' said Costa, 'leaving out the war period.' He turned down the corners of his mouth, feeling that a sympathetic grimace of contempt was expected of him. He had no intention of explaining to Calles what it was like to be a single victor among the defeated.

The lieutenant found some difficulty in deciding what to say next. He had prepared a subtle line of argument with which to gain Costa's confidence, as a preliminary to enlisting his co-operation. But such a course of action seemed shameful in the light of the discovery which he had made. Although Calles was never at a loss for words in pursuing professional ends, he had little experience or practice in the ordinary sociable trivialities, when the roles were not that of interrogator and victim.

'You know, Costa,' he said, 'in a way, I still feel as though we were in enemy territory, you and I. We're running our personal cold wars, the pair of us. Don't think I'm not aware of the way you've been victimized. We need each other's support now, perhaps even more than we did at Teruel . . .' He checked himself. Quite unintentionally he found himself slipping into a professional tone. He glanced at Costa anxiously.

'Be sure that anything I can ever do, sir,' Costa said, feeling that something, he was not sure what, was being asked of him. With the strengthening of the lieutenant's friendliness, a suspicion had dawned. Costa thought, that's the way they always go about it when they're after something. I'm not joining his Gestapo, if he thinks I am.

At Teruel together, Calles was thinking. There was no stronger bond he could imagine. He wanted to do something to make the occasion seem more comradely. 'Do you drink?' he asked. 'I'll send a man out for something.' The lieutenant, who for many years had smiled only with his muscles suddenly bared his teeth engagingly, in a further effort to put Costa at ease.

Costa stiffened. He was certain now, and all he wanted to do was to get away as diplomatically as possible. 'If you don't object, sir,' he began, '. . . it's more a question of time. There was something I had fixed up to do. . . .'

The lieutenant was understanding. 'Of course, of course. I understand perfectly. You have your work to do, and it won't wait. But do promise to come back soon.' He searched Costa's face almost pleadingly. 'We've a lot to tell each other about old times,' he said. 'Any time you're at a loose end, you know. Without putting yourself out. After five is always best. Make it tomorrow if you like.' He got up and held out his hand.

Costa mumbled his thanks and a farewell in an unfinished phrase in which he was able to avoid definitely committing himself to a further visit. They don't credit you with much intelligence, he thought, as he went out. You can read them like a book.

There was an ancient bed-ridden woman propped up at the window of the house opposite, her old yellow face invisible in the darkness of the room behind the glass pane. Even the passing of a dog was a noteworthy incident in this emptying life and, when Costa came out into the street, she said to herself; there he comes, now, and all dressed up to kill. In there a long time. What a man his daddy was, and to think that I'd only to say the word. And now he's gone, and there aren't any more like him. Never have been any more since he went. Wonder what his boy would have been doing in there all that time.

Costa went down by the beach again. Now the wind had plucked the clouds from the mountain tops, teasing them into a sky-covering of thinnest wool. It tinkled in the bead curtains over doorways, and raised small blizzards of fish scales about the market. Costa observed these things with concern, noting, too, the spray-softened outlines of the cliffs, and the sea moulting its white feathers into the sky where the horizon had come very close. As he had feared, there would be no visiting his lines that afternoon, and if — as was possible — the big fish had been hooked two nights before, it might now be dying. And if on the following day the sea should still be too rough for his small boat, then putrefaction might set in, so that on the fourth day the carcase would be unsaleable. These were the real, the cruel risks of the fisherman's life. It was like one of those dice games, full of ingenious hazards. You had to throw a six before you could start, and then before you knew where you were you landed on a snake's head, and were back at the point you started from.

Standing there, Costa was under observation by four men sitting at a table in one of the sea-front cafés. Two of these were the men he had passed in the street on his way to the barracks of the civil guard and had later seen again in the orderly room. The others were Francisco and Simón.

'And what makes you so sure, for instance,' Francisco said, 'that he wasn't there for the same reason as you were?'

'By his manner; by his hang-dog look, if you like. Look here, Francisco, if you're called to the police-barracks to be fined or beaten up, you don't bother about who sees you go in. You go in and get it over and come out.'

'He was just going in,' said the second man, 'and then he saw us coming. He was like a cat on hot bricks. What sort of interpretation would you put on that?'

'It all fits in with what's been going on,' said the first. 'It makes sense now. You would have thought he was the lieutenant's brother, the way the corporal spoke to him. Listen, have you ever noticed that special kind of voice that the civils put on when they're not talking to anyone like you and me? "Would you mind stepping up to see the lieutenant, sir?" I can hear him now . . . Mind you, as far as I'm concerned, there was no proof needed. I've known it for months.'

'Known what?' said Francisco.

'Well, you'll admit that someone's been giving us away for months on end now. Who else could it be?'

'We've got to get rid of him now,' said the first man. 'We can't afford to let the thing go on like this.'

Down by the sea wall Costa blinked as the first rain stung his eyes. The landscape had drunk up a little of the sky's silver, and the wind, tearing at the edges of the advancing shower, spattered the men who were watching him with a few drops.

'There's not a scrap of real evidence against the man,' Francisco said.

'You have only to ask yourself who could have given Pedro away that time he got it in the neck for the overloaded boat. There was only Costa there to see him come ashore.'

'And then what about the two fellows who took out

trippers without a licence? They wouldn't go with Costa because his boat wasn't big enough.'

'There's one thing I'm still not happy about,' Francisco said. 'This applies particularly to you, Simón. It's your personal attitude that comes out all the time. Don't you think it's about time you made an effort to forget what's past and done with?'

Simón turned, his face suddenly contorted as if by a spasm of unbearable agony. 'Forget, did you say? Wait a minute now, before we go any farther, let me ask you something. Do you see that thing down the road, there?'

'What thing?'

'The thing. That's what I prefer to call it. War memorial, if you like.'

'Well, what about it?'

'Have you ever gone to the bother of reading what it says?'

'Many times.'

'And do you remember now?'

'I suppose I do. More or less.'

'I'm word-perfect. It says, fallen for God and Spain. After that comes a lot of names. Are your brothers among them?'

Francisco made a face of gentle exasperation. 'What's the point . . . ?'

'Neither are my sons, who died of wounds in the camp without receiving the last sacrament. Didn't they die for Spain? Didn't they die for God, too? What right did the people have who put up that stone to decide who died for God? Why try to make up God's mind? Why not leave it to God, to decide who died for him? I believe my sons died for God.'

Francisco was thinking: there's no end to this, it just goes on and on. Simón said: 'Do you know, sometimes I'm afraid I'll get woolly in the head. I'm terrified of forgetting. We all get old. Then I say, thank God for the memorial. I'm grateful to it. Let no one ever remove it. While it's there I'm safe from forgetting. That's your answer.'

The storm put an end to the discussion. Rain splashed down on the men's cheeks and fell on their hands like tears of anguish. It stood in great quivering drops on surfaces of brick and plaster, and lizards zigzagged through them escaping to their crevices. The streets emptied and soon the children came out to sail paper boats down bubbling brown torrents and to chant a joyous song about some ancient tragedy turned comic in the race's memory.

CHAPTER 17

COSTA watched the rain spend itself and the colours leap from the landscape as the sun edged out of the clouds. Then the wind blew itself out — the brief, empty bluster of the storm overwhelmed in summer. He stayed out for the rest of the day, mooching about by the shore, watching the gradual sinking and smoothing of the waves, wondering how heavy would be the swell that would certainly come riding in from the deep sea on the morrow, and whether the boat would be manageable in it. He was full of forebodings.

He waited to go home until the pines had speared the last of the brightness out of the evening sky. His old mother was in the courtyard preparing the evening meal.

'You're back then,' she said. 'How did it go?'

'Not so bad,' he told her. 'Nothing to worry about, anyway.'

'Just settle yourself,' his mother said. 'It'll be ready in a few minutes.' He caught the sickening odour of the arañas boiling in the pot.

'I don't feel particularly hungry,' he said. It would have needed something more than araña to stimulate his appetite after the excitements of the last few days. He felt unable to tolerate the suspense of waiting for the next day. Twelve hours divided him from the action of the next morning, and he could not imagine how he would use them up. Now, also, as the uneasiness arising out of his visit to the police subsided and ceased to distract him, the great underlying anxiety about Elena floated up to the surface of his mind. That evening the promised letter was to be delivered, and Costa knew that when it came he would be afraid to open it.

'What did he want?' his mother asked.

'What did who want?'

'The lieutenant.'

'Nothing. He wanted to have a chat with me. That's all.'

'Well,' she said, 'that's something new at least. The first time any member of our family ever went to see the police without coming back poorer than when they left.'

'It was all right,' he said. 'Nothing at all, in fact.'

'What did he have to say?'

He tried to escape her by opening a cupboard and raking about among some of his fishing gear, but she was insistent and he knew that he would have to make a small surrender of truth to her.

'Well,' he said, 'if you must know it was something to do with the army.' He was hastily preparing his half-admissions knowing how an accurate report of their conversation would sound to her suspicious ears.

'The fact is,' he said, 'we happened to be at Teruel together. You know — the time they put all the fellows like me they weren't too sure about up in the front line. I told you about it before . . . where I caught a packet, before I managed to wangle out of the infantry and get a job in the supplies.'

The ones they weren't too sure of . . . knew they couldn't trust us any farther than they could see us . . . always the well-worn self-justifications which she had forced herself to believe in the way an intelligent child will cling doggedly to a belief in fairies.

'Did he ask you to spy for them?' she suddenly said.

'No,' he said, 'of course he didn't. He was pally like you are when you've been in the army together.' Costa stammered a little, caught suddenly with the necessity for another self-justification. 'I mean how was he to know that it was no fault of mine that things were as they were? Had to use my head all the time or they'd have put me against a wall.'

The old lady went for the cooking-pot, moving with the slow, calculated movements of her age, thinking once again how strange it was to be taken so unawares by the bodily weakness which the years had brought, while her brain remained as nimble as ever.

'You'd better eat,' she said. 'Tomorrow will be a hard enough day for you.'

She went away again and brought a bottle of last year's wine, sweet, thick and cloudy, but rare in their house. He was surprised. She settled down at her end of the table. He took his fork and a piece of bread and broke the sodden white flesh of the fish away from the backbone. 'Aren't you going to eat?' he asked, looking up. She shook her head. The light was very dim now. He wondered what she was thinking about and was a little disturbed that the questioning had stopped, leaving him with his little stock of unused prevarications.

Having come to a decision, the old lady felt the need to glut her eyes with familiar objects. She got up and switched on the light. Everything stood in position, emerging obediently under her direct scrutiny from habit's mantle of invisibility: the beautiful things out of reach on high shelves, decorated pitchers and flasks that use had never profaned; the photograph of her husband, vague as a ghost with over-enlargement, clownishly hatted by the photographer; an ikon of Saint Peter, promoted by the reverence of those who followed his trade to a Spanish knight in armour; a crucifix in a gilt case, the Christ broken away from the cross and tumbled among Roman soldiers who were turbaned like Moors. ('Just leave it to me,' her husband had said every second or third day for ten years, 'I'll put it right tomorrow.' Thus the shrine had acquired a second sanctification — to a beloved habit of procrastination, turned by death into virtue; and she never saw the small, sprawling, dusty figure of carved bone lying there at the bottom of the shrine without feeling her husband's almost physical presence.) Each bare room in this house in which she had lived for over fifty years had come to contain its little kernel of magic and holiness.

In this moment, too, in her eagerness to fix every detail of her home in her memory, she heard the swallows for the first time, twittering a little in the eaves before night silenced them. They had always been there, a part of all the summers of her life. But now for the first time she separated the sound from the others, setting it aside in an effort of memory, because it was one of the sounds of her house.

'Let's pack up and go to Puerto de la Selva,' she said.

Costa felt a stroke of incredulous joy.

'You mean you'll come, too?'

'Next week's the anniversary of your father's death. We'll go after that. What use would you be without me?'

'You mean you'll settle down there? . . . leave this place for good?'

'I don't feel like staying here any longer,' she said. 'You'll want a few days to get all that stuff down from the store. A good thing I saw to it that the nets were repaired before we stowed them away. Your father was very careful with his things. You'll find most of them as good as when he bought them.'

'You really want to go next week?' he said.

'That depends on you,' she said. 'As soon as you can find a house, I'm ready. Just give me until the Friday.'

'There's something I forgot to mention about Elena,' he said. 'When we were discussing various things the question of Puerto de la Selva came up.'

'I suppose she wouldn't raise any objection to marrying you so long as they didn't happen to hear about it in this place.' The old lady summoned a little cantankerousness to her aid against the sadness rising up to choke her.

'It wasn't ever a question of that. It was the money,' Costa said. 'She'd have married me any time if I could have made enough money to live on.'

'Money,' his mother grumbled on, forcing back her nostalgia, 'in my days, there was never any money. I remember a time when for four years running there were no sardines and the men had to go to work as labourers. They were so hungry they used to ask the farmers to bake pine branches with their bread, otherwise they would have eaten the whole day's ration as soon as they got it in the morning. Do you think that nobody got married then?'

'She didn't care about money,' he said stubbornly. 'If it was anybody's fault it was mine.'

In these matters there was a barrier of reserve between Costa and his mother. It was in some way unmanly to lay bare deep feelings for a woman before a third person, even a parent. Mutual tolerance, even indifference—these were for decent public exhibition. Speaking of his relationship with Elena, Costa felt obliged to undertake a laborious mental translation, search after cautious and bloodless words to interpret the ardent thoughts. So all he could say now was: 'On the whole I'd just as soon stay where we are if Elena didn't feel like coming, too.'

This amounted to the only declaration of his love his mother had ever heard him make.

Costa pushed back his plate and went and stood in the doorway, the fish-smell cut off there by the sharp odour of potted geraniums. He stood there while a greenish residue of daylight poured out of the sky beyond the western hills. Black shapes of men moved past silently on their rope soles. He heard a murmur of sweet-shallow music from the theatre tent at the other end of the village, the dogs yapping and the slow, heavy breathe-in and breathe-out of the rollers coming up the beach. The curve of the village round the darkness and the sea showed in pale squares diminishing to dots. Above, where the night thickened over the mountains, the points of a few charcoal burners' fires pricked through the gloom.

'Señor Costa, I've something for you,' the small, hooded form of the postwoman had materialized before him, a dark wedge in the white fishbone silhouettes of rigging. Costa took the letter, whispering his thanks, and slipped it into his shirt so that his mother should not see it. He sensed bad news. And if there were bad news, his mother's questionings and her solicitude would be unbearable to him.

In his room he tore open the envelope, and took out the three sheets of coloured paper smelling faintly of soap, covered with the big sprawling, backwards staggering handwriting, his fears deepening because Elena's letters never consisted of more than a couple of sentences cribbed from the models of the professional letter-writers, revealed nothing, only served to confirm her recognition of the bond that existed between them.

'Esteemed Friend' (all the little manuals on letter-writing counselled a prudent mode of address), 'Permit me to excuse my failure as a correspondent by reminding you that my duties allow of little leisure to attend to personal affairs.' His eye rushed on past the standard opening sentence. How little of the heart's yearnings and fears would seep through to reach him past this close filter of set phrases!

'I was unable to converse more freely with you today because we had no time, you must have thought me strange Now I have given consideration to the matters under discussion and I want to leave here quickly I've had enough of it but I can't leave because of some money I owe So the fact is I must have a thousand pesetas I did not wish to inform you about this but you said about going to Puerto de la Selva So I was trying hard while we were walking about all that time.' At this point the writing got worse, the big round letters crumpling in deflation, the words beginning to run into one another. Costa held the sheet closer to the little lamp, screwing up his eyes.

'If I could have the money by public messenger on Thursday it would be all right but not after then It would be unnecessary to trouble yourself I am sorry to ask you to lend me this money because I have no right to ask you.'

Here Elena had written 'Believe me As ever Your sincere friend who clasps you by the hand', but she had crossed this out and added a P.S.

'If you can find the aforementioned money by Thursday I will come back there if you like or we will go to the other place you said about Money must be to hand by stated day because Friday is my day off for month and I must have it by then If unable to do this I may be able to see you again but I don't know.'

Squeezed into the bottom corner she had written, 'I send you a tight hug,' which she had never written before. As usual there was no signature.

Costa re-read the letter twice, searching for hidden meanings, finding the second reading more frightening than the first, and the third reading still worse. She must have stolen from her employer, he thought. Perhaps her father's sick again. There was no knowing what anybody would do once they were exposed to the big town's infection. The evil of the city was recognized by all toilers of the land or sea as limitless. People forced to live there for only a short time were prone to undergo a kind of bewitchment, from which they recovered as soon as the municipal duties shed, erected at the town's outskirts, was passed on their way back. And if Elena had caught the city's sickness, it was no more her fault, he thought, than if she had caught the smallpox. Removed to Puerto de la Selva in its clean wind-swept bay under its corner of the Pyrenees, she would instantly recover.

She's pocketed some money, that's it, he concluded, and what they'll have done is to give her until Friday to pay it back, before handing her over to the police.

And now it was Tuesday night, which left him with no more than one clear day, to find the money before the messenger left on Thursday morning. A thousand pesetas. Only twice in his life had he possessed so much money. On five times that amount a man could get married decently, but it took several years full of good luck to collect it. For half that sum you could be buried reasonably well, although after twenty years, if no further contribution was forthcoming, your bones would be removed from their burial niche to make room for others, and thrown into the common ossuary. A thousand pesetas. Costa wondered how long he and his mother could live on so vast a sum on their diet of arañas and black beans, supplemented in winter with the acorns which he collected in the woods. The next-door neighbour had been lying in bed for the last three months waiting to die for want of a thousand pesetas to pay for an operation. There were ten beautiful girls about the village who would be betrothed the day their fathers could mention a dowry involving such a figure.

Old as the boat was, it could be sold, and probably for a thousand pesetas, but the thing needed time. People didn't buy a boat every day of the week, and when they took such a step they were likely to insist on a week's trial, and then a few more days of indecision while they chewed the thing over with the old uncles and aunts in the background who would be sure to be financing the project on a catch-sharing basis. Apart from the boat, there was his fishing gear. It could be sold in the village at a knock-out price, or in one of the local towns for something near its worth. But that meant coming to an arrangement with someone with a lorry, paying him in advance for his petrol and, even then, perhaps waiting a few days before a buyer turned up.

And then Costa remembered the great fish in its submarine cavern, fifty kilos of it at least, and worth all of eight hundred pesetas in the prevailing seller's market. Here was the answer to his problem, and the more he thought about it the more certain he was that the fish would be hooked by now. With the fisherman's invincible superstition that always lies in wait to ambush his reason, Costa now saw this episode of the big fish as fore-ordained, the deliberate intervention on his behalf of fate that so long had fawned dog-like at his heels, and then, after capriciously deserting him for fifteen years, had perhaps given this as a sign of its renewed favour. The next day he would go out again, strong with confidence, and wrest from its lair the splendid prize that awaited him, and with this he would ransom Elena from the cruel servitude of the city.

So that night he slept fairly peacefully, not even hearing as he usually did the soft unlatching and closing of doors when Molina came in.

CHAPTER 18

FOR the first time for many months, Molina's habit of falling asleep at dawn was broken. After half an hour of listening to his breathing, Paquita slipped out of bed, wiping away in the palm of her hand the sweat where their thighs had touched, and pulled her dress down over her head. She switched on the feeble lamp and examined Molina's face. With the ebbing of his vitality he had gone cadaverous, cheeks collapsed, mouth open and askew, the teeth cleansed of their discoloration by the yellow light. Molina's mind burrowed eagerly back into a fantastic version of childhood, while his breath rattled noisily through his throat, and a mosquito fed quietly on his forehead.

Almost as a matter of habit, Paquita slipped her hand into the inside pocket of the coat hanging over the chair, removed the wallet she found there and began to count the notes. Not much of a man at all, she thought. But at least he was a cut above those glassy-eyed shopkeepers who crossed themselves before getting into bed with her, and then behaved as if they were semi-finalists in some sort of competition, to say nothing of the old sparks who couldn't manage anything until they had her acting like a performing monkey. Not much of a man certainly, but one who, Paquita's instinct told her, was like herself, up against it. Twelve hundred pesetas, odd. She put the notes back in the wallet, and the wallet back in the pocket. After all, she might as well have been his girl friend, the way he had treated her. 'Feel like going to bed? If you don't, it doesn't matter. Some other time. Not keen? Of course I'm keen. What do you imagine?' Sometimes you had to make a gesture, whatever it cost you. Gestures were what distinguished the salt of the earth, like Pépé, from the rest of humanity. Let him keep his money. Every peseta of it.

And now, the gesture having been made, the little question cropped up of how she was going to eat next day. She took the torch that stood against the wall by the head of his bed and went up on to the roof, glad to escape from the damp-hot, poverty-stricken, cat-stinking smell of the room, and of the whole house. On the roof she was part of the night, the cool flowing night, that gave its creatures absolute freedom of the world.

She found the handle of the roof store, went in and switched on the torch. Paquita knew by experience that the fisherfolk stored away the bric-à-brac of generations in such places. Here would be found the broken clock, the silenced musical box, the stringless guitar — valued, sentimental, forgotten trash whose absence would never be missed. But here there seemed to be less hope than usual of discovering any small piece of loot that her friend in the junk-dealing trade would buy for a tenth of its value plus his discretion. She wandered about poking among the piles of nets, fingering the old acetylene lamps, testing the points of harpoons. A polished turtle-shell took her eye. She was impressed by the picture in a mother-of-pearl frame of a dark-faced Spanish saint slaying infidels, and enchanted by a schooner in a case miraculously modelled out of sea-shells and coral. This treasure, which she supposed to be the compensation for the hardship of living in houses, she reluctantly abandoned, as being too beautiful to be of value. Here the only clock had been emptied of its works, and she was just about to give up her search when she happened to lift the corner of the sail and found the wireless set. At first she was doubtful whether it was worth taking. There were few impressive knobs, and no engraving. Then she picked up the head-phones attached, critically scrutinizing their curved plastic surfaces and chromium plating, and thinking: surely this must be worth ten pesetas of anybody's money?

So she pulled the set out of its hiding-place and, finding a length of cord, tied it up and carried it to the edge of the low balcony. On one side of the house an Italian bomb had left a square of desolation holding broken brick, the polished, negroid limbs of cactus, and a little moonlight. Into this she most carefully lowered her find.

Just before the night lifted, clean-edged as a drop-curtain from the sea, Paquita went to the house of a man called Pablo and awakened him by pelting his bedroom window with handfuls of small stones. Pablo was an ex-politician who after a lifetime of manœuvrings and manipulations had secured a parliamentary seat as an independent radical, on a programme of advanced social reform, just before the outbreak of the National Movement had abolished parliamentary democracy. Since then he had turned his back on ambition. In the summer season he now earned a sparse living by standing absolutely still for three pesetas an hour, got up to look like a dummy, holding a menu outside the local hotel's restaurant. Apart from this he dabbled in smuggled birth-control requisites, and for a modest fee would occasionally castrate a horse.

Pablo came down and let Paquita in. He jostled panting up the dark staircase after her, hoping for a brushing contact with her body on the narrow turns. When they reached his living-room, he fell into a chair, winded. He was over seventy, grey-faced, carrying laboriously, on short, weak legs, the body that had been designed for a successful bourgeois. 'My dear little girl,' he said, 'how good of you to come to see your old friend!' He felt a little sick from his exertion and, pulling an end of a nightshirt out of his trousers, he dabbed at the cracked surfaces of his blue-grey lips.

Paquita put the wireless set down on the table, and Pablo, recovering, prodded at it with slightly flattened fingertips.

'And what, might one ask, is this museum-piece — an electric-shock machine?'

Paquita said, 'It's my boy-friend's radio set. You know, the one I told you about, who's doing time. And allow me by the way to tell you it's one of the latest models. He bought it in Cadiz only last year. You can get Venezuela on that set.'

'Interesting,' Pablo said, moving round the table towards her. 'I should have said it was a bit of an antique like myself. They haven't made them with earphones, as far as I know, for the last twenty-five years.'

'Do you want it or don't you? . . . And get away from me, you old monkey.' Pablo, who had been trying to look down her neck, drew back hurt. Sniffing, Paquita scanned the room contemptuously, seeing the sacred picture with the dying flowers beautifully arranged beneath, the crockery greasy with the remains of the last meal. 'This place stinks to high heaven,' she said. 'Why don't you risk opening a window?'

'We've known each other long enough to be perfectly frank, dear,' Pablo said. 'I must admit your contraption doesn't interest me at all. Naturally I'd like to do something for you as a dear friend.'

'I know you would,' she said, making a mouth of disgust.

'As it happens, I wasn't referring to anything but financial aid. I'd help you if I could out of sympathy, if you can understand what that means, but I'm cleaned out. I've had to give up working at the hotel. My feet were swelling up so that I couldn't persuade my shoes to go on ... Really now, how much do you need, dear?' He leaned over and reached for her, and she slapped his hands away.

'A hundred,' she said, 'and that's the fifth part of what it cost.'

He went into another room, came back with a small roll of dirty notes, and counted out fifteen single pesetas. He put the notes down one at a time on the soiled tablecloth, where they lay there curled like autumn leaves.

'What's that for?' she said.

'There's such a thing as real sympathy, dear child,' he said, 'but alas, what's the use of trying to explain things which by their nature are beyond the reach of your comprehension. Being human I'd make it twenty-five if...'

‘Who, you?’ she said. ‘Well, Christ! just imagine that.’

‘Take the money, then, dear, and go in peace,’ he said. ‘One day I’m afraid you’ll come to the knowledge of what it is to be old, though be sure I don’t wish you such a thing.’ He looked down at the massive wreck of his body, which trembled a little on the thin, worn-out legs, and his eyes watered unseen in the dim light. ‘There was a time — ah well — the heart’s still there. Still in the right place. Come back any time, dear. I’d love to see you, if only for a chat.’

Paquita screwed the fifteen notes into a ball and went out without saying goodbye.

CHAPTER 19

WHEN did I eat last? Paquita wondered. Yesterday, was it? Yes, of course, the thin chap stood me a meal. Just as well, after all, I didn't take his money. Even Pépé would have looked down his nose at the idea. She remembered the time when, risking his neck as a bandit, he had held up a car-load of farm hands on their way to a football match. 'Pile out there,' she could hear him say, from where she was crouching behind a tree. 'Now turn out your pockets, and throw the stuff on the ground.' They had twenty pesetas between them, and he made them pick them up again, and then gave them another hundred to spend with his compliments. Forced them to take it. What a man! He couldn't help putting on an act, whatever it cost him. Now she came to think of it, Molina and Pépé had something in common. She couldn't put her finger on what it was, but Molina reminded her of Pépé. Perhaps she would run into him again later in the day. She hoped so. What a good thing she had kept her hands off his money!

And now she had fifteen pesetas to last her until God knew when. And she was hungry. That afternoon she would have to drag herself through the matinée routine. She would go through two singing and two dancing numbers with an audience of seven or eight adults, and the front row full of grubby, chattering, apathetic children, sent there to be out of their parents' way. The total take would come to about fifty pesetas, and one or two people would be certain to demand their money back because all the numbers had not been changed since they had last seen the performance the week before. Whatever the receipts, they would all go to pay for the lighting, and the two-man orchestra, who also worked as scene-shifters and would only stay on the strict basis of a daily wage.

After that, Carmen, who was fond of saying, well at least she had never sold her body (but didn't object to cadging from those who had), would start screeching that her milk was drying up, and Fernando, who found women difficult to get because of the tube in his stomach, would try to worm himself into her good graces by passing round the hat to buy Nestlé's to feed the kid. Then there would be quarrels about the order in which they came on, and about taking curtains — they would go on quarrelling over things like this when there were more performers than audience. One of the girls would kick up a shindy because Antonio, the flamenco dancer, had helped himself to her powder again, or was wearing her corset; and there would be moans of 'Why the hell don't we get out of this — make a move — go to some other place?' ('Because we've no money to buy petrol, let alone get the car fixed up, you fool.')

God, what a life! she thought. What a lousy life! I've got to have a square meal to face another day of it. With something inside me perhaps I won't feel so bad.

She went into the Twentieth Century and snapped her fingers in the direction of the morose old waiter.

He came up reluctantly. 'Were you wanting to order something?'

'Well, you don't suppose I wanted to sit here and hold your hand? What's on the menu today?'

'Rabbit.'

'Do you recommend it?'

'All I can promise you is, it's not cat. Apart from that anyone will tell you the rabbit's the most syphilitic of all the animals.'

'All right,' she said. 'I know all about that, and anyway, I'm not so sure. How much is it a kick?'

'Eight pesetas.'

'Robbery, I call that. Barefaced robbery. What's the portion like?'

'Giblets and ribs,' he said, looking over her head at the cruel pockmarked satire of himself shown him by the ruined mirror. 'The limbs have all gone.'

A party of foreigners had come into the café and were eyeing her with admiring curiosity. The girl of the party, who was unhappy because she had just discovered herself to be in love with her divorced husband, cheered up a little and said: 'I think she's quite wonderful. She's serene. I mean she's got a kind of—well, serenity.' She was anxious to prove that she had the generosity of spirit to praise another woman's beauty.

The man thought it politic to be critical. 'Oh, I don't know, dear. Of course, if you admire that particular type—but there's only one woman in this room who fits that description for my money.'

She looked him in the eyes, shaking her head, realistic and brave, ready with a revealing glimpse into the profoundness of her character. 'I'm not serene, dear. Perhaps I used to be, but I'm not now. You see, I've lost my serenity. We all do.' She took his arm impulsively. 'You know, it's just as if they still had the secret of something we've lost.'

Paquita, staring back at them, was entranced by the girl's neatness, her small, delicately carved, mask-like face, the gaiety of her clothes, and above all by the pale, short-cropped hair. If only I could be like that! Suddenly she was conscious of the drabness of her own appearance. Her self-assurance faded. She felt swarthy and unkempt.

'Well, what's it to be?' the waiter said. 'There's only twenty-four hours in one day.'

'Look here,' she said, 'Do me a favour, and bring me a glass of water. I'm not hungry any more.' Paquita had remembered that Calles would be waiting for her, his lust fanned by the days of anticipation. At any moment now a message would come from him, and she must be at her best, the nearest that by the grace of art she could approach to one of these pale, tranquil, self-assured goddesses. She would stake her precious fifteen pesetas in the throw. It was worth it. A drastic change in her appearance might just be enough to tip the scales with the lieutenant.

Five minutes later she was back at the theatre, changing into the blue jeans which someone had given her the year before; and then, with her morale half-restored, she went to the hairdressers.

'I'm fed up with this hair-do,' she explained. 'I want something more up to date. Less of a mess, if you know what I mean.'

'A cut with the ends neatly permed, perhaps,' the hairdresser said. His eyes lost their focus picturing the tame-trimness of the result of this sabotaged luxuriance.

'How much will that set me back?'

'Thirty pesetas.'

'What else could you do with it, for about half that much?'

'In that case I should favour a wash and a set, with a chignon.'

'I'll take that, and see how it looks.'

An hour later the drier was taken off, and she saw the result reflected in three mirrors; the tight cone of hair in the nape of her neck, which arose now clearly revealed from the uncovered duskiness of her shoulders. She was quite calm. 'Run a comb through it,' she said.

'I beg your pardon, miss.'

'Take it down, I don't like it.'

'You mean put it back as before?'

'That's right,' she said. 'Just as it was.' I'll never be like one of them, she thought. I'd have to cut it off altogether, and then dye it, and even then, I can't dye my skin.

'If the style wasn't satisfactory, miss . . .' he began, but she cut him short. 'It's me that's wrong, not the style.' She gave him the fifteen pesetas and went out, feeling quite cheerful again, and just at that moment a civil guard came up and said: 'I've been looking for you everywhere. The lieutenant wants to see you.'

'Where are we going?' Paquita asked the man.

'To the barracks,' he said.

'To the barracks? I thought for reasons of his own it wasn't convenient,' she said. 'Didn't he tell you?'

'Those are my orders.'

Funny, she thought. The thing had gone the way she expected. Quicker even than she expected. She'd given him another few days to hold out. But why the barracks, then? Anyway, she was glad to be all dressed up for the occasion, and her hair smelling nice, even if it was half way down her back as usual. Anything Calles had from her he was going to have to pay for, if she knew anything about it, because she knew that, when the puritanical ones like him fell they fell harder than the rest. If that didn't do the trick for Pépé, she would give up. It would be hopeless. He would have to stay where he was. She was done with being a stool-pigeon and getting nothing out of it.

As they turned in to the barracks, she stuck her hands defiantly into the pockets of the jeans. Clothes like that gave a girl a feeling of poise and independence. From now on she would wear them all the time. Going up the stairs she was humming 'My Horse's Bells', the number she had brought the house down with in Valencia. 'All right,' she said to the guard, 'I know my way up. See you later,' but he insisted on sticking to her, just as if he were bringing in a prisoner.

When she went into Calles's office, he was sitting there bolt-upright behind his table, with a new expression on his face. There was an even stronger whiff of disinfectant than usual. 'Hullo, handsome,' she said. She sat down in the only comfortable chair and crossed her legs.

'Stand up,' Calles said, in a matter-of-fact voice, as if commenting on the unseasonable weather.

'What on earth for?' she said. 'I'm tired.'

'Stand up,' the lieutenant said again. She stood up,

noticing with a cold little shock of recognition that the bulky object on Calles's table was a wireless set.

'You've been busy, I see.' The edge had gone out of the lieutenant's voice, and it was over-pleasant and at the same time confident in a way that was new to her. Calles had always seemed a little confused in his manner on the occasions of their previous meetings.

'Where did you get the wireless set?'

'From a friend of mine.' She tried to be casual, but her shallow, speeded-up breathing was betraying her. This was a bad start if she hoped to make any impression on him that afternoon.

'Name and address?' Calles asked, his eyes never leaving her, sketching idly as he spoke on a blank sheet of paper.

'Couldn't tell you. Just someone I happened to meet.'

'Why did he give you the set?'

'For services rendered, if you like.'

Picking up a fly-swatter, the lieutenant annihilated a fly that had alighted on his desk. When he turned to her again she had the impression that he was gazing at her like a jealous lover.

'What services?'

'Why press the point?' Through her fear, she felt her annoyance growing.

'Do you know something? I don't believe you,' Calles said. His smile was like the result of a fairly successful plastic operation.

'All right then, I found it on a rubbish dump.'

'You found it on a rubbish dump? Of course. Good.' The lieutenant nodded, seemingly satisfied, relieved even.

'A rubbish dump,' he repeated quietly. He reached out and pressed a bell, and an enormous guard came in.

'Ribas,' he said, 'this young lady's not being exactly co-operative. Put her over the table and give her a dozen of the best.'

Ribas looked at Paquita uncertainly for a moment, and Calles seemed to interpret an unspoken question. He nodded at the jeans. 'Oh yes, you can take those things off.'

And this was what he had really wanted of her, she knew now. The excuse to torture her. This had been at the back of this unnatural and sinister calm of his. He was confident in the knowledge of being within reach of his objective. And to think that she had imagined she could ever win over this beast with her love. Ribas's iron hands were tearing at her clothing, smothering her struggles as if she had been a child of five.

'Where did you get the set from?' Calles's voice was indulgent, almost caressing.

'Go to hell!' she told him, half choked by her struggles.

Calles said: 'I think one thing should be made clear. I'm not in the least interested in whether you stole the set or not. It's the man you stole it from who interests me, and you won't leave this room until I know his name.'

The guard held her now with one huge hand pressed into the bare flesh of her back, holding her pinned down like a butterfly on the table's surface. She was exhausted. 'All right,' she heard Calles say, 'as soon as you're ready.'

They're after some poor devil, she thought. Perhaps it's the thin chap. But I'm not giving the game away, not if they beat me till they're blue in the face. I hate them so much. I won't give them anything, and they won't beat it out of me. I'd sooner die. How much pain can I stand? Never had a baby. Abortions are all that my kind can afford, and they're bad enough. Abortions, toothache, a broken leg as a child, and once a knife through the hand; not too bad, any of it, all bearable. The abortions were the worst. Supposing it was even two or three times worse, she could stand it, without giving them the satisfaction of letting them hear her yell. 'Carry on,' she heard Calles say, and biting into the flesh of her forearm she began to count, one, two, three, four . . . by the time I reach twenty it'll be all over, and then as the hosepipe smashed down on her buttocks her mouth opened wide, and with all her lungs and with vocal chords that had suddenly broken away from her control she screamed.

'Mother — mother — mother — mother — mother.' They were crippling her, she was dying, all her life was blotted out by this one terrific experience. Between the blows consciousness went away only to come back in a great sickening, on-rushing wave. She retched, but nothing came from her empty stomach but a dribble of bitter liquid.

'Put a newspaper under her mouth,' Calles said. 'I don't want a mess.'

If only they would let her stop screaming, she would tell them anything they wanted. Struggling for the breath that her screams were consuming so fast, she began to choke in her own bitter vomit. The blows stopped. There was a raging silence through which she slipped into a dream. Then she was awake again, hearing a voice which she recognized with a shock of surprise as Calles's, saying: 'Well, now that that little unpleasantness is over, perhaps we can get down to business without any further waste of time.'

CHAPTER 20

WITHIN an hour of Calles's telephone call the car carrying the special police, which was elaborately disguised as a taxi, came roaring down the hill into the village and pulled up outside the barracks. The over-polite chauffeur climbed down and opened the door for the three unmistakable men, dark-suited, a town polish on their shoes, their faces weighted with smiles and melancholy, who had sat there stiffly upright throughout the journey. The three men patted the dust from their clothes, glanced patronizingly at their surroundings, and at a sign from the chief, who was dressed in mourning, went up to Calles's office. The driver climbed back into his seat, pulled down the braided cap over his eyes and, shifting the pistol which pressed uncomfortably against his hip, went off to sleep.

Calles received them like a fencer on guard. All three men declined to sit down, watching him with eyes a little aslant in faces blood-leeched by their profession. They had brought the atmosphere of an investigating commission into the room with them.

'And what measures, may we say, have been taken so far?' asked the man in the black suit. He spoke sternly as if the measures and blunders amounted to much the same thing.

'Our first move, when we found the man was not there, was to put a corporal in the house opposite to keep the place under constant observation.'

The man in thc black suit raised his eyebrows. 'In plain clothes, I sincerely hope?'

Calles said: 'In view of the fact that all our men are well known in the village it seemed a useless precaution.'

'I hope it occurred to you to put the occupants of all houses in this street under house arrest?'

'That was done immediately.'

'The people with whom the wanted man was lodging ... you have their statements?'

'The woman's deposition is here. Her son is still out fishing.'

'And how can you be certain that the son is not involved?'

'He happens to have the best political record of any man in the village. Besides that, we've established that it was a pure chance that the wanted man went there in the first instance.'

The man in the black suit frowned. 'If you'll permit me to say so, you seem to be ready to take a great deal for granted. I take it you've every egress from the village under observation. I say *every* one.'

'Yes,' Calles said, 'every one.'

'You see what I'm getting at of course. We've got to see to it that nobody gets the opportunity to warn the fellow — which they will, if given half the chance.'

'Quite so,' Calles said. He would have given a great deal to know the rank of this man, and wondered whether it might not have paid to have started off by addressing him as 'sir'.

His interrogator picked up a small volume of the *Way of Perfection* of Saint Teresa, looked at the title, sniffed, put the book down and wheeled round.

'All boats confined to port?'

Calles risked a thrust. 'There's no port here. A few inlets, that's all.'

The man in black showed his irritation. 'Come, lieutenant, don't let's quibble over words. You know what I mean.'

'Half the boats are still out. I've got men down on the beach. To sum up the situation, no one can get in or out of the village, by sea or by land, without our cognizance of the fact.'

'I devoutly hope so,' said the man in black, shaking his head.

One of his subordinates took advantage of the pause. 'Perhaps we might see the man's foreigner's registration form?'

Calles opened a folder and took out a small oblong sheet. He had passed every obstacle so far, but was still on his guard. The three men inspected the paper gloomily, unable to find fault with the way the entries had been made.

'You know, lieutenant,' said the chief, 'for the life of me, I can't see how you let this man practically slip through your fingers. His description was sent out to all departments months ago.'

Calles, tight-lipped, quenched a smile. Another paper came out of the folder. 'I have the description here — "Man, age about thirty, weight seventy-nine kilos, black hair" — shall I read through the rest? He's five years older since then, going grey, and weight down to sixty at the most.'

'Don't think I'm sitting in judgment on you. We're

here to see that the thing's not hashed up from this point on. Let's hope we're not wasting our time, because my feeling is that as soon as our friend found his transmitter gone, he took to his heels. The safest bet is that one of my people will pick him up somewhere between here and the frontier.'

Calles said, 'And you think he'd be likely to leave his money and his passport behind?'

'That does give us a grain of hope, I admit. But to come to the important point, I can't emphasize too strongly that this man must be taken alive. We don't want him dead. He's no more use to us as a corpse than his weight in mutton. If you think that it's asking too much to try and get this into your men's heads, then they're to patrol with side-arms only. I warn you that there'll be as much of a fuss made if some moron puts a bullet through his head as if he gets clean away. That's clear, isn't it?'

'Perfectly,' Calles said coldly. 'Fortunately, other ranks in the civil guard are in the habit of carrying out the orders they receive.'

'I'm glad to hear it,' said the man in black. 'Picking the man up's your job. After that we can start work . . . By the way, while we're about it, I may as well have a few words with the old woman.'

'She was allowed to return home.'

The three men exchanged horrified glances. 'You didn't hold her?' said their chief incredulously. 'Am I to suppose that that's your usual practice?'

'In view of the woman's aged and feeble condition, I considered it unnecessary,' Calles said stiffly.

CHAPTER 21

SINCE childhood the world had shrunken, and then, at first unnoticed, it had stopped shrinking and begun to expand again, until now in old age it was infinitely immense. Roads lost themselves in horizons once more limitless, but devoid of adventure. Hills had swollen into mountains, and woods thickened into impenetrable forests. Stony, impassable places had appeared in streets once smooth. Cactuses struck out with spines like daggers, and flowers grew out of reach.

Marta went down the village street, watching her footsteps, picking up out of habit the little offerings of shade. The doors were shut and the swifts overhead screamed in and out of the great, waiting silence, which was like the silence that precedes the first shots and screams of a revolution. There was a single painter with sun-flayed back under a Mexican hat, who was trying to put on canvas his tranquil holiday sensations, and who wondered why there were no children looking over his shoulder. A yellow taxi turned the corner and came towards her, its headlamps blinking in the sun, and she saw the three city-blunted profiles of the men who rode in it.

The last of the houses of the poor breathed out their odour of rancid oil upon her, and she reached the first of the summer villas, where a fat, lethargic boy, who had been stalking goldfinches with an air rifle, stopped for a moment to regard her with mild aversion. She began to climb the path which was one of the five ways out of the village. It was narrower and steeper than when she had last climbed it ten years before, and the brambles were more tenacious, but Molina had told her that his favourite walk was along the cliff top, and by now, wherever he was, he would be making his way back to the village for the meal of boiled fish which she had ready for him in the late afternoons.

This, she said to herself, was Sebastian's doing. A pat on the back from the lieutenant, and a little soft soap, and he'd been ready to play their game. Sebastian had always wanted to be thought well of, to be on good terms with people, to cut a good figure. You could flatter him into anything. As a child he had scandalized them all by announcing that he was going to be mayor when he grew up. He might as well have said cesspool-emptier for the impression he had made. There was something presumptuous, cowardly, and a little ridiculous for a son not to want to follow his father's calling. It turned out, on questioning, that Sebastian had noticed that people like to shake hands with the mayor, and on Sundays the men raised their hats to him on their way to church. So in the end he had persuaded them to give him a little extra schooling, and he had been asked to carry a banner in the processions, and had shown people how to fill in their tax forms. But when the office of mayor had fallen vacant, they had elected a taciturn ex-goatherd who was offhand to his supporters, and returned, it seemed, almost thankfully to his old profession when the change of government automatically removed him from his position.

Marta turned a corner, and there was the civil guard, day-dreaming behind his dark spectacles, lonely and off-colour, protecting in the cup of his left hand the illicit cigarette. The alsatian with him came up at a heavy, padding trot, then, catching the scent of her inoffensiveness, turned off.

'Where are you off to, mother?'

Her heart was beating too loudly, and she was a bad liar. Marta believed that when a man put on this uniform the devil granted him a diabolical insight into human motives. She waited a little till her breath came.

'Up the hill to see to some bees.'

'Bees is it?' he said. 'How many bees, and just whereabouts?' He was bored and homesick, and his mind was elsewhere. He asked questions, mechanically, from force of habit, but Marta, dry-mouthed and silent, knew that he had seen through her.

'In any case, it can't be done. Come back tomorrow.' The guard stuck the yellowed stub-end back between his lips, dismissing her with this gesture. His mind went away from the present, groping backwards. Let's see, there was something pleasant I was thinking about. Can't remember what it was, but it was a good thing to think about. Was it about women? It must have been about women. It was pleasant, too. Why the hell can't I remember?

Marta went down the hill again, easing her body step by step down the slope. There were four other paths to be tried, but each one was sealed off by a man in uniform who was either trying to count the trees in a distant hillside, or watching a beetle roll a ball of dung uphill with his back legs, or gnawing the heart out of an unripe fig, but always keeping alive that grain of alertness that was sufficient to record the approach of anyone that wanted to pass that way. The draining away of Marta's strength prevented her carrying her search into the village itself, but had she done so she would have found a plain-clothes policeman sitting behind the door in each of the cafés, while another strolled with fungus-pale skin and borrowed costume among the visitors on the beach.

At four in the afternoon, Molina, who had been sleeping quietly in the woods, was awakened as the shade dipped away from him, and a shaft of sunshine, unrestrained by a coarse mesh of branches, fell upon his face. Making his way down to the main road, he was picked up by a Frenchman in a large, smooth, luggage-piled car, and given a lift back to the village. No one recognized him. In response to a guard's signal, the driver slowed down, but was waved on again. When Molina saw the old woman dragging herself along on the last stage of her homeward journey, he asked to be put down. 'Run for it,' she told him. 'Drop everything and run for it. The police are here.'

He did not understand, and stood there smiling and apologizing for having kept her waiting for the meal. She clawed at him unable to make him realize the crisis, because no expression of urgency could show through the aged mask of her face, while her voice was always high and sharp-edged. Neither could Molina understand the Catalan into which, in her excitement, she poured all her thoughts.

But at last one word came through, 'police — police — police,' and with fatal seconds squandered he understood, still paralysed by uncertainty, his face gone old. The clatter and scuffle of hard boots at the end of the street, and the shrilling of a whistle awakened him.

Molina ran twenty yards blindly, not thinking of where he was going but only of getting away from the whistle, and then there was a uniformed man at the street's corner towards which he was running, and he was trapped with shouts and the whistle-blowing again. He doubled back, frantic as an animal bolting from the slaughter-house, bottled up, low walls closing him in, but with no footholds, no way — since he was no athlete — of getting on to a roof. Then as he ran and turned, and ran again and turned, a door opened and he went through into the darkness of a house, and then into the light of a little courtyard, and through the open door of the courtyard into the overgrown waste land beyond, where the slope began that steepened into a cliff.

He went up quickly, tearing himself through the bushes on the first easy gradient, and then clambering foot by foot, slipping, sliding and crashing down as his feet dislodged loose stones, and the bared roots he clung to ripped away under his weight. At last he could climb no higher, with a hundred feet of perpendicular cliff above him, and the courtyards of the houses below, first empty and then slowly filling with upturned faces. He began to work his way across the cliff face towards the sea which was very close.

There were shouts below, now, and then a sound as if a cow was straying in the tight, dry growth of bushes, and Molina saw the dog coming up. It came through the bushes with a dash, shoulders hunched, head down, wavering a little as it followed the exact trail of the sweat-scent he had left. Molina's blind flight was halted at the sight of the dog. He hated it and the new emotion steadied him. The dog came on, muscled like a lion, leaping obstacles with calculated bounds. I must have time to think, he said to himself. At least a few moments to think.

A little below him and to the right was an outcrop of solid rock with a smooth face, about five feet in depth, and a flat top on to which he could clamber down. He reached this platform, just as the dog, following his scent, was coming up from the left, and calling to the dog, as a bull-fighter calls to the bull, 'huh! huh!' he made it look up and change its direction, heading straight for him where he stood on the rock's top. Just below the base of the rock the dog sprang, but the slope was too steep and it was going too slowly, a little winded from its climb. It landed with its forepaws over the rock's top, and its hind legs scuffling for a purchase, and Molina kicked it with all his force under the jaw, sending it rolling back fifty feet down the steepest part of the slope.

Below someone shouted: 'Tell that fool to call his dog off. Is this what you call discipline? I want a megaphone to talk to the fellow. Has no one a megaphone?' Two policemen with a rope approached the edge of the cliff and were waved back.

Molina was carefully edging his way across to the steeper part of the cliff face and the sea. He was calmer now, and was trying to think of resignation. This is the moment you are supposed to have trained yourself for, he was thinking. So now compose yourself. How often had he pictured himself looking into the muzzles of the rifle of a firing-squad! He was sure he could have done it. No last cigarettes, no nervous gestures of defiance. No useless self-consolation of shouted slogans. Molina had planned to die in a calm silence, mind withdrawn, his dignity unimpaired by emotion. And now the time had come, and surely it was better to die at the moment chosen by himself, in the light of the day, and with hands untied.

Why am I trembling? he wondered. Perhaps because I've been running away. While you were still running it meant you still had hope, and it was hope that made the coward. Was there any justification for hope? He looked up and then down. None at all. No hope. Finished. Face it then. Face it, face it, face it. Resignation was the only prize now, the only objective to be gained.

Another five minutes, something within him implored. Only another five minutes. It was the wrong time of the day to die. You died at night, or at dawn, prison-weakened, a bit drunk if somebody took pity on you, in the unreal greyness of some courtyard, having gone through the various processes of despair, the world already as good as lost. But here the day was real and the world more solid than it had ever been before, with his finger-nails full of red earth, a cloud of bright bluebottles buzzing round him, the stink of a seagull rotting on a ledge a few feet from where he crouched, the cheerful permanent sea awash below and a single big cloud coming up from the south, which would take longer time than he had left to reach and cool the sun. I'm going to die now, he thought, accept that. No village in the Camargue and no neglected postmistress with no dowry, also no grave, and no one to say how he had gone, for whatever that was worth.

The crowd had increased. 'Clear all those people away

immediately,' said the man in black. 'Do they think this is a Punch and Judy show? Is that megaphone coming, or isn't it? If we make the slightest false move, we're going to lose this man.'

'He's as good as lost, already,' Calles thought. 'I've seen this happen before. Sometimes it takes them five minutes to make up their minds, sometimes half an hour.' He saw Molina move again, edging across the cliff face to where there was a sheer drop. 'Go and get a boat out,' he said to one of the men, 'and look lively. He's going to jump into the sea.'

Molina was thinking: 'Why am I still here? What am I waiting for? I'm weakening. I'm trying to trick myself. In a minute I'm going to manufacture some sort of excuse to let them catch me, so that they can torture me into working for them to set a trap for the others. No, they're not. Oh, no, they're not. But I'd like to have finished one or two things, and there's someone I would have liked to say goodbye to. I wonder how long they'll remember me? It would have been easier to have gone out if they could have seen that I did it the right way. Funny to worry about things like that when you're on the point of dying without any belief in anything in particular. What does it matter what they think, or how long they remember? But it does.'

He had come a long way along the cliff from the village, and there was water among the rocks beneath him. The clean edge of the cliff towering above the village had been shattered here, and the man with the rope stood staring down across a chasm fifty yards wide towards the spot where he had last seen Molina before he vanished from sight. A few tiny figures had detached themselves from the crowd and were struggling away in search of a better viewpoint. Two guards, crossing the neck of the headland, had reached the next inlet where the boats were tied up, and were receiving slow and surly co-operation from a fisherman who had been ordered to put his boat in the water. Molina never doubted that it would not be long before a boat arrived. Ten minutes, fifteen minutes perhaps; but no longer.

He looked down. The rocks below were ugly and jagged, iron-red above the water, and a pale drowned colour beneath. Molina could not bear the thought of the hardness and the sharpness of the rocks. Looking down again, he felt a fluttering in his stomach. Painfully he edged his way farther and farther along the ledge until he reached a place where it jutted out over the water. From here there could be no more retreat. Sharp-edged stacks riven from the cliff face had slid down to wall off his path. What does it matter? he thought. I shan't know anything about it. He found the phial and shook the two pills into the palm of his hand. They were white, glossy and odourless. Molina tasted one with the tip of his tongue. It was sweet. He roared with laughter. The funniest joke in his life had come to its end. Sugar-coated suicide pills! . . . If only they could provide you with the pangs of death on the instalment plan. He put both pills into his mouth and, with a little difficulty, swallowed them.

The faint sound of his laughter, breeze-carried to Lieutenant Calles's ears, confirmed his pessimistic surmise.

'What's he up to now, sir?' the corporal said.

'You'll see in a minute,' Calles told him. And as he spoke, as if in response to a signal, they saw Molina drop, half turning in the air before he was lost to sight behind a knuckle of boulders at the cliff's base.

CHAPTER 22

THE new day was breathless although the sea still moved with the pulse of forgotten storms. Costa rowed strongly after his rest, following a line drawn from headland to headland, past beaches laid down like ceremonial carpets in the fresh light, and cliffs rearing up from a drifting incandescent spray raised like dust-motes from the broom of a vigorous sweeper.

Nearing Moors-in-Hell his confidence began to waver and he challenged his good luck to compete with him in childish games in which the odds were always arranged in his own favour. If I see three seagulls before I reach the next headland, the fish will be there all right. There were plenty of seagulls about but, when in the given time only two appeared, a distant white bird which was almost certainly a pigeon was accepted as a substitute. It was unlucky to consider the mere possibility of failure and the exact nature of the crisis which might be expected to result from it.

Costa had been born into a society with the richest traditions of superstition. Throughout the ages the fishermen had made a kind of subconscious and ill-organized investigation into the nature of the gods of good and evil fortune, who made so many dramatic entrances into their workaday lives, and they had come to a rough agreement on what could be done about them, which was very little. Unlike the Virgin of their religious faith, who was human by instinct and impulse, these deities were unapproachable. No prayers, and no chanting, no offerings of candles or flowers could mollify their ferocious caprice, and only by treading carefully could one avoid the worst pitfalls of offence. There were three unlucky actions: wearing foot-leather, whistling at sea, carrying a priest in a boat, and it was easy enough to keep these in mind. But there also existed a supreme omen of their disfavour about which there was nothing to be done — the fox — whether glimpsed slinking from the scene of its morning slaughter, or as a fur on the coat of a fashionable visitor, or even the mention of its name. That night, foxes had come to Costa in his dreams, pouchy-cheeked, grinning, ready to devour his luck. Costa was trying hard not to remember this dream.

He found the spot where the line had been set and put out his anchor. The boat swung gently in polished hammocks of water. He reached out, hooked the cork-float and drew it in, hauled up the heavy stone that anchored the line and dropped it into the bottom of the boat.

Now he began reluctantly to pull in the line itself. Six metres came in slack, Costa pulling more and more slowly, and then he stopped, frightened. The hope of a better life, even the continuance of this existence he had come to terms with, depended upon there being a fish. He did not want to go on pulling in the line. Don't think of the foxes, think of the Blessed Virgin. He held the slack line in his hand and tried to concentrate on the Virgin of Mercy, honorary mayoress of the village, her swarthy, good-natured doll's face peeping out from the stiff brocade as she was carried in the processions, or even on her picture that was stuck on the back of the village barrel organ. But the face of the image would not come and the fox-faces that were sent by the heartless arbiters of abundance and disaster were real with the reality of nightmare.

He took the line and began to pull in again, suddenly weakened by fear, and then, just as the weakness and trembling of his limbs went to his stomach, he felt the line come alive, first leaping stiff in his hand, then lying slack, then snatched away again, then taut and lifeless with the dead resistance of a fouled anchor at its end. Costa stood up in the boat, opening his mouth as if to shout with relief, yet ashamed, although the sea was empty, a curtain of ashen water hanging from a knife-edged horizon. Now the day was changed, electric, perfumed, unveiled. Through the silk-rustle and cough of the sea in the caves he heard the small birds, who wound themselves up in all the cliff-bushes, release their brief clockwork songs and ran down. The foxes had gone, and when he tried an optimistic experiment the image of the Virgin was there, bobbing along benignly in her throne above the heads of the crowd.

Costa leaned over the side and took the line between finger and thumb. He tugged very gently, feeling the line give in its length, and feeling the distant muffled scratching of its fouling the sharp rock-edges. The rock's sawing at it in at least two places, he thought.

He found his diving goggles, spat on the insides of the lenses, rubbed the spittle round with his finger, rinsed the goggles in the sea. He put on the goggles and then the lead-weighted belt with its cork-hafted knife in sheath and lowered himself over the boat's side. Filling his lungs he folded his body at the waist and kicked up his legs, and the water closed over his head silencing the day, cutting off a seagull's whimper, and as the lead belt drew him down the monstrous beauty of the underseas took shape about him.

Fish moved away with dreamy undulations behind veils of blue water, and where the sea's bed sloped into the depths others, catching the yellowed sunlight as they turned to feed, flashed distantly like the beams of far-off lighthouses. He sank quickly, head-first, following the line, with the water's iron fingers in his ears, and his limbs weighted with watery grace. The rocks opened and passed him on all sides, blind prison walls, yellow and sea-smooth or lava-wrinkled, nourishing gardens of grey blooms, their foundations screened in languid weed threaded through with stealthy fish-movements.

Costa followed the line into a cave opening. Light sliced through a crack in the further wall and shattered into a yellow haze, through which small fish span away like silver coins. He took hold of a rock-spur and pulled himself into the cave. Sea-anemones in the narrow opening touched his limbs with their infants' mouths, and coralled edges slashed at him painlessly. Now having observed the position of the crevice into which his line disappeared he pulled his legs under him and, doubling his body, kicked out forwards, thrusting his head back through the cave's mouth, face up and eyes on the distant dimpled-sheeted silk of the sea's surface, brown blood smoking from his cuts and the beginnings of the drowning agony in his chest. As he went up, flattened silver balloons of air squeezed through his lips and went rocking past his eyes.

He caught hold of the boat's side and hung there for a long time sucking in lungfuls of air. Then he hauled himself into the boat and lay down in its bottom, the hot wooden surfaces soothing the chill of the water and the smart beginning in his cuts and in the places where sea-urchins' spines were embedded. Dreamily he began to plan his next move. In the old days he had trained himself to dive sixty feet after coral and lobsters, but the dive into this cave which was in no more than half that depth had tested his endurance. He was out of condition, short of breath, flabby in the muscles that this called for, and his ears hurt him badly. With every dive he would come up more exhausted and, becoming tired under the water and with his judgment failing, he would be insensible to the slashing and grazing of his flesh by the sharp rocks. But he was never for one moment in doubt that some time that day, early or late, he would break surface with the big fish.

In his first dive he had resisted the chill of the stagnant depths, but diving again he felt himself break through a surface of icy water lying just beyond the spear-points of the sun's warming rays. Bitter currents entwined in the acid-green of the weed enveloped his limbs, and a cramping cold seized his loins as he slid through the cave's mouth. A black fan spread at the crevice's opening suddenly closed and was whisked from sight. Plunging in his arm, he received a heavy blow on the wrist and felt a great waterlogged thumping commotion, like the convulsion of heavy machinery swamped in an inrush of water. Excitement anaesthetized him. He no longer felt the cold or the savage pain in his ears.

He clutched out, found his line and pulled and the convulsions died away, as if in doing so he had switched off some source of power. He slid his hand up the line and found the crevice completely blocked with a slippery polished mass, steel-hard at first touch, ribbed and strutted, and then betrayed by the soft circle of a great eye which rocked to his prodding finger, and the down-drooping rubber softness of the huge blubbered mouth. Parting the lips he felt the line, frayed thin where it passed through close-clustered needle teeth. Now he drew his knife to grope for the two small targets unprotected by the armoured bone. At that angle the knife would not enter the eye, but there was an inch of throat uncovered, and as he stabbed the point struck on a hard surface, slipped a little and went in. Six times he buried the blade, feeling each time the unflinching firmness of the flesh on his knuckles, as the fish faced the knife, gills expanded by iron muscles to hold it firmly in the crevice.

Costa's lungs were beginning to pound. He began his retreat, extracting himself with wearily-desperate gymnastics. For a moment he was trapped in a green iceberg, released to pain by the passing of the emergency, ears bursting and mind wandering a little. Then he went up into the warm bath of the surface water.

He lay in a sort of coma until past noon, roused and lulled by the trivial noises all along the shore, the bland tilt and fall of the boat, the sun's lick. Sometimes drowsily he saw the sky, deepened to violet, between the lash-bleared slits of his eyelids. The small hermit-crabs which he used for bait scrambled up boldly from the boat's bottom and crawled teeteringly over the backs of his hands. A mild kind of beetle called a Pharaoh's-mask blew over and, dropping like a minute helicopter, tasted the drop of blood that had oozed from his ear.

He awakened with spray in his face, and the sea fresh and dark and white-toothed, flouncing before the breeze, and the new impatient waves slapping into the boat. To deaden the cold he put on his vest and shirt, tucking the shirt-tails under his belt. This time he wanted to reach the cave more quickly, to save every second of his lung capacity, so when he dived he was holding two heavy links of an old anchor chain, to be released when he reached the bottom. He went down blindly through a foam of bubble-filled water, swirling away from where the waves were pounding the rocks, into the tranquil depths, and the shrill cold and brilliance of the undersea's arctic night. Within seven seconds of leaving the boat and with thirty seconds in hand he was in the cave, the centre of a planetary motion of small curious fish, his arm in the crevice, feeling for his line. In the past hours the merou would have pumped out its small supply of blood in a thin, constant trickle, losing most of its strength with the bleeding. But even when in mortal agony, drained of vitality, virtually unconscious, it would go on fighting, with a will to live unequalled among the warm-blooded animals of the earth.

Costa found the line, pulled and felt the dead resistance. He pulled harder, doubling with his exertion the rate of oxygen-exhaustion in his lungs, and the line gave a little with the faint jarring of a ruptured strand. Unable now to risk a further strain on the line, he wrapped it once round his left wrist. Bracing himself with his knees and with his left shoulder he found the fish's eye with his right hand, plunged through his index and middle fingers and hooking them behind the socket gave a tremendous tug. Costa felt the fish give way, coming out with a sudden smoothness as if from a greased socket, barrel-huge, mouth gaping, monstrous in its toad-hideous beauty. There was a tremendous, wrist-breaking convulsion. Costa felt as powerless as if he were trying to check the onrush of a bull. The fish struck him full in the body, carrying him right out into the main opening of the cave. In desperation, Costa let go the hand holding the line and thrust the fingers through the other eye-socket, grotesquely embracing the fish which stabbed at him with its sharp-strutted fins, the huge hopeless mouth agape held close to his, ruby-red throat pulsating. First Costa and then the fish was uppermost, as it strained with body muscles and thrashing tail to throw him off. But in its blindness it allowed itself to be guided through the cavern's opening, and it was at this moment that Costa's ear-drum burst and the sea revolved, so that he was looking down into the foam-roofed surface, and carried struggling down, still embracing the fish, into the boiling light where the waves buffeted the rocks. He never had any recollection of reaching the boat, nor, when he thought about it later, of how it was he managed to get both himself and the huge fish into it.

CHAPTER 23

THE darkness had thickened, but Costa could make out the position of the creek below the village, from the glare of the acetylene lamps on the sardine boats as they came out and went away, slowly burning their path over the black water.

Until the night had covered it, Costa had never taken his eye off the fish, watching with affectionate interest the small details of the last hour of its life; the colours extinguished, the last tremors of the gills, the jaws' final snap, the glazing of the ruined eyes. There it lay with a little of its blood, dry and dark, painting the wood beneath it, and a few scales, shed in its last fury, stuck like a decoration on the planks, What a fish! he thought. A hundred pounds, at least. Perhaps a hundred and ten pounds. He would never catch or even see the like of this fish again. There would be a sense of loss in giving it up, in seeing it pass from his ownership into profane hands, to be divided by the desecrating knives of those who knew nothing of the drama and mystery of its catching. Had the circumstances been different, Costa would have kept the fish for at least one whole day in the refrigerator at the market, to prolong this happy sensation of possession, and to give the whole village time to gaze upon it respectfully. But there was no time. As soon as he got to the market he would be obliged to summon the three women who were the regular buyers, and conduct the auction, and within three minutes the thing would be at an end, the money paid over, the drama concluded. He could see in his imagination the faces of the three black-draped, fish-reeking harpies, who would bid against each other, their professional grimaces of depreciation for once in conflict with their amazement.

Seven hundred pesetas. This was the value he put on it. Perhaps a few pesetas more, allowing for the summer visitors in the village who could be made to pay through the nose for fish of exceptional quality. The buyer, whoever it was, would cut it up and make a profit of three hundred — enough to keep Costa and his mother for a month out of this one and only slice of good luck. The buyers always took a share of your good luck, but left you to get on with the bad by yourself. If they'd had any sense, they'd have organized a co-operative long ago, he thought, to cut the buyer out — but there it was. Anyway, say seven hundred pesetas at the least; and with this sum in his pocket he would go and find Molina, and with profuse apologies, and giving him some inkling of the urgency of the situation, would ask him for a week's money for his board and lodging in advance. Nine hundred and fifty pesetas that made, plus the household's cash reserve, which he was certain amounted to at least the remaining fifty. By ten o'clock that night, which was the time at which he closed his office, Costa would call on the public messenger with the packet containing the money, sealed in half a dozen places, and Elena's name and address carefully printed on both sides, and the messenger would give him a receipt and lock the packet up for the night in his safe. And then Costa would go round to the doctor's and get his ear seen to.

His ear could wait until then. The sharp, throbbing, iron-boring pain had subsided into a bearable ache, and the chill of the evening had revived him. Costa rowed on, his strength returned, until the last black silhouette which had screened the creek's entrance lost its shape and slid past him. A boat was coming out with lamps aglow and, on an impulse, Costa steered towards it, hoping that the men might have the chance to see the fish. For a moment he was bathed in a yellow glare, and then the boat was past, riding in its luminous, brilliantly blue patch of water, and carrying away with it the row of curious, then averted faces. Even if they didn't see it, they'll hear all about it tomorrow, Costa thought.

There were a few half-employed boys, just past the school age, loitering in the spread of light from the boats down by the water's edge. Costa called out: 'Anyone feel like making a peseta or two? I want a hand to carry this fish up.' There was no reply, and the boys drifted away back into the darkness again as if no one had heard.

Carry it myself then, Costa thought, and lucky to have the chance to do it. Somehow or other he got the fish on to his back, with arms bent back over his neck and fingers hooked in the gills, and began the slogging climb up the beach. His feet dug into the wet sand. Wherever he could, he stopped to balance the fish on the edge of a boat and rest. The thin, polished bone of the gills' edges began to cut into his finger joints. Something popped in his ear, releasing a little trickle of warm blood.

This was the hour when the village, which by daylight had a drowsy, half-deserted appearance, came alive. People having no immediate work to occupy them made a point of coming out for an evening promenade along the main street or down by the water front. Most social activity was squeezed into this cool interlude between sunset and the final meal. Girls, strolling in twos and threes, offered themselves in a depressed marriage market. Well-to-do visitors who would take their evening meal late walked fairly briskly to get up an appetite. Fishermen, who had already eaten and would rise while it was still dark to spread their nets in advance of the dawn movement of fish into deep waters, made the most of their sparse leisure. Down at the fish-market they clustered sociably about the empty slabs where the fish were sold by auction as soon as they were landed. Odd catches were offered here at all hours of the day and night, and such was the fascination of their calling for them that fishermen who were resting could think of no better place to while away their time than here, where they could keep an eye on what the sea had to offer.

The three buyers, Engracia, Lola and Lucia, waited in their houses, the slaves of their thirty-three and a third per cent, doomed to be perpetually on call, and attuned to the condition of the market by complex grape-vines of intelligence. For thirty-three and a third per cent they were expected to spring from their beds at any hour of the night, and arrive at the market within five minutes of the landing of a catch. It was even said that thirty-three and a third per cent had induced Engracia, who combined avarice with piety, to leave instructions that she was to be called from Mass when catches amounting in value to more than ten cases of sardines were offered.

On this particular evening Engracia was engrossed in

her favourite pastime of cutting the obituary notices out of the newspapers which she bought in bulk to wrap up fish, and sticking them in a book. 'Fell asleep in the Lord,' that's nicely put . . . still when a man's been a Companion of the Congregation of the Most Holy Sacrament. And I must say I prefer disconsolate to afflicted — there was a sharp rapping at the door. 'Who is it? Coming, coming. Don't be so impatient.' She threw open the door, spilling weak light on the face of the man who was standing there. 'Good evening, Simón. Anything worth having? If it's another half-basket of mackerel, I don't want to hear about it.' Simón came into the room without waiting to be asked. 'Something I want to have a word with you about — do you mind?' He closed the door and, while Engracia looked on in wonderment, leaned down and shot the bolt.

By the time Costa had manhandled the fish as far as the market place, he was in a bad way again. The small lounging group divided to let him through, and he flung the fish down on the slab, and straightened himself, gasping, to await the accolade of their astonishment. They gave no sign of being aware of his presence. Marco — one of the men who had shown him such remarkable cordiality on the previous day — stood only three paces away, and now slowly pivoted till his back was turned. Exhaustion soaked up most of Costa's bewilderment. A few boys filtered through the indifferent gathering to peer into the fish's gaping jaws, relaxed in death, or to risk a quick prod at the scale-armoured flesh. 'Hey, you Fernando!' Costa said to one of them, 'go and find out if the buyers are coming, or not.' Really it was unnecessary, because they would be already on their way. He sat down heavily, half collapsing on the slab beside the fish. Fernando looked round uncertainly and then went off, hands in pockets, kicking at invisible stones.

Doctor Rosas was passing as he had done exactly at that time, and with the same two friends, for the last five years. He had just been displaying a new possession, an inscribed cigarette lighter. 'And as I was saying it's their freshness of attitude that enchants me. Imagine me, for example, trying to steer the conversation in a certain direction. I let out a bit of a sigh and make a grab for her hand, then I say: "Romantic here, isn't it? Get's under your skin, so that you always want to come back." "It would be more romantic still," she says, "if the lavatories flushed occasionally." See what I mean about the fresh outlook. You haven't seen it that way before.' He broke off. 'Excuse me, I must have a look at that fish.' He went over to Costa. 'Hm. And very nice, too. Much of a fight? You seem to be rather battered.'

'I believe my ear's gone,' Costa said.

Rosas went closer and peered at it. 'No doubt about it. Rupture of the diaphragm. Simple enough if you look after it. Better have a wash up, and come over to the surgery.'

'Thanks,' Costa said. 'As soon as I've got this fish off my hands, I'll come up.'

Rosas took his wrist. 'You're dizzy, aren't you? Can't even stand on your feet. No pulse worth speaking about. The fish had better wait.'

'I'm all right,' Costa said. 'I got here under my own steam.'

'You see what I mean,' Rosas said to his friends. 'That "I can take it" attitude. They're like that. And then they get an infection that puts them on their back for a month, and it's a case of "Why didn't you tell me, doctor?" '

'Have it your own way,' he said to Costa. 'You're on the verge of collapse, whether you know it or not. Well, it's your funeral if you go and knock yourself up.' The three men walked on. 'Medical science is wasted on them,' Rosas said. 'They'd walk about on a broken leg if they thought they could save ten pesetas that way.'

Costa, aching and impatient, saw the boy he had sent to call the buyers. 'Didn't you tell them to get a move on?' But the boy said something he did not catch and pushed away, his face a little wolfish with embarrassment, to join in some horseplay down the street. Costa shouted after him, the pain leaping up in his ear at the effort. He put up his hand and brought it down blood-blotched.

One of the men spoke for the first time, talking away from Costa. 'He says they're all out.'

Somewhere in space a voice said, 'Engracia is called urgently to the bedside of her dying sister. Señora Lucia's brother-in-law took her by car to Barcelona for the christening of their child.' Costa turned his head, and a third voice at his shoulder, as if catching him off his guard, said: 'Lola the fishwife has a threatened miscarriage.' The voice went on, continuing a conversation in which Costa was not included: 'Poor creature, not allowed to stir from her bed, even to answer the call of nature.'

Costa pushed himself to his feet and moved forward on uncertain legs, disconcerted at the way the men drew back and moved aside to let him pass. Lola the fishwife lived just across the street from the market, so that she was usually first upon the scene when a catch was spread out on the slab. Day or night he had never known her door to be shut before. He rattled the handle, kicked at the door and shouted through the keyhole. There were heads at all the windows. Half a dozen children who had followed him stopped cautiously in the middle of the street. The men at the market-place stayed where they were, throwing him over-shoulder glances. He rattled at the door-handle again, and there was a noise of shutters being opened overhead, and an elderly woman with a grey, wrathful face came out on the balcony and said: 'Do the favour to make less noise, when there's illness in the house!' He turned away and the children scattered as he had seen them scatter at the threats of the imbecile who sometimes broke out of the upstairs room where they kept him locked up, and went with genitals displayed, mouthing and capering down the street.

Costa reached the slab and, catching the fish by the gills on each side of the head, lifted it up. He stood there for a moment totally bewildered, with no idea at all what to do next. Then suddenly the answer to the problem was there. He had seen Cervera, the controller of the municipal refrigerator, moving, an elusive shadow, at the back of the crowd. Dropping the fish on the slab again, he went after him. 'Hullo there, Cervera! Hear about the fish I caught? Quite a battle, I can tell you. Look here, old son, it won't be convenient to sell tonight, so we'll just pop it in the 'frig till tomorrow, if that's all right with you.' If the worst came to the worst he would collect his money in the morning, drag himself somehow or other the six miles to the junction with the main road, and get a lift in to Barcelona.

Cervera, a good man, showed a strained face; a small, sad, cornered Pontius Pilate. 'Oh dear me, well now the fact is . . .'

'I want to get away to the doctor's and get myself patched up a bit. Don't want to rush you but you can see how my ear is. My head's going round in circles.'

'The fact is . . . didn't you know . . . there's no ice because the plant broke down. You see it all depends on the plant, and it broke down — well — precisely for that reason there's no ice. Not a cubic centimetre in the place. I mean that's the situation in a nutshell, the plant not functioning and consequently no ice.'

Costa's lips moved, as he tried to form words.

Cervera said mournfully: 'We can put it in the box. Yes, by all means. Here are the keys; you see I carry them about with me. The large key is the one to the refrigerator. There's no trouble at all in opening up. Don't think that. Only without ice, you see, it would be as high as mutton by the morning.'

A moment of ringing silence passed over Costa's head and Cervera spoke again as if in answer to some objection that Costa had not made. 'I agree that the sardine boats are out, but then all catches will be taken, if God's willing, to be sold at Puerto de la Selva.'

Inside Costa's head a horizon of consciousness rotated, and suddenly he felt the black gush of a river somewhere, through cresses and pebbles, at the back of the night. A Moorish tower subsided its day's hairbreadth, shaking down a little powder. The food in the bellies of the men facing him squeezed forward an inch in its progression through the intestines. There was something painful he had forgotten about.

A little too much music had been stirred into the air, and was now falling here and there, like drops of reluctant summer rain. The pattering of the music strengthened, and something swung back smoothly into position in Costa's brain, as he recognized Cañadas, the hotel's factotum, who was coming towards him, playing a guitar. Cañadas, who had become the shadow of a fiction by setting himself the task of living up to what he believed to be the hotel guests' expectation of Spain, was on his way to serenade a party of young ladies lodged in the evil-smelling rooms known as the hotel's annexe. He stopped, shook the frustration out of his face, and trilled a few bars from Verdi. 'Hullo, all! The top of the night. What's going on here? Speak up or for ever hold your peace.' The fishermen looked through him. Costa was at a circus with white horses going round at a canter. Suddenly a fox leaped on to the back of each horse. He reined his mind in, but the earth still tilted.

Cervera, uneasy of conscience seized his chance. 'Any chance you could do something with a nice fish? You see how it is; if we could keep it overnight, all well and good, but the refrigerator's given up the ghost.'

'A fish now. Oh, my God!' Cañadas said. 'I've been offered some funny things in my time, but this takes some beating. What is it — a young whale?' Tiny bull-fighters moved, bracing themselves for the onrush of their adversary as the breeze caught at the carnival shirt he wore.

'I don't say for your own purpose,' Cervera said, 'but for the hotel. After all, it makes a change.'

Calculation had strengthened Cañadas's shiftless face. 'Sorry, and all that, but the budget's settled for the week. Soon see you haven't much of a clue on how to run an hotel.' He turned to Costa. 'I'll tell you what. If you can't get shot of it, come and see me. I might give you a hundred or so for it. Better than nothing, after all.' He struck a few chords from the guitar and was moving off when he found his path barred by the fisherman Francisco. Francisco was dressed with dark, stiff-jointed formality, as if for a wedding or funeral. A little yellow light clung to the smooth protuberances of his face where he had just shaved. 'We don't allow thieving under a different name,' he said. 'If anyone wants fish they get it from the buyers at the proper price, and, if the buyers don't want it, that's their business; they've got their reasons.'

The other men were drawing away, abashed, unsaddling themselves of the responsibility of the moment, and, as Francisco went on speaking, Costa revived as if a bucket of water had been emptied over his head—heard what he knew to be the passing of judgment upon him.

'Why can't we speak our minds? I don't know, I'm sure. Farces like this don't do any good. Let's get it off our chest. If the buyers won't buy this gentleman's fish—well, that's it. The fish isn't for sale here. He can go and sell it somewhere else. That's the remedy. And you can go and buy it there, if you want it.'

Costa would have killed him if he could, and gone gladly to the garrotting post, but, although his brain was working lucidly again, all the power had left his limbs.

I'll kill him all right, as soon as I can pull myself together, he thought. Break his back over the gunwale of his own boat. And any of the rest of them I can get my hands on while I'm about it. And then finish myself off.

He stumbled forward, hands raised, and broke easily through the cordon of watchers, but at that moment his brain revolved again, and he was among the windmills, shivering from the breeze raised by their sails blowing down on his unprotected skin. He was searching for something — urgently, desperately, impeded in some way by the pain in his head, which flowed out continually to colour the poppies in the cornfields. A time limit, too, had been set to this hopeless mission, because the sun was going down fast, and soon it would be dark.

As Costa went running and stumbling up the street, they followed him; the children first, close behind and cautiously cruel, and then a few of the younger undisciplined men, and a galvanized mass of evening idlers, who only knew — but without any of the details — that someone had gone crazy. All the responsible fishermen, members of the fraternity, had made themselves scarce, driven from the market-place by Francisco's angry glances and gestures.

The market-place was deserted and the big fish lay there lessened and shapeless now, dissolving away into its own shadow cast from the light of the single small lamp. For five minutes the half-silence of cicadas and distant dogs was undisturbed and then a great misshapen cat dropped from a wall, light-footed as a ballet dancer.

The cats of Torre del Mar were no ordinary members of

their species, but a specialized race of carrion-eaters, tolerated as scavengers, developed here through the centuries since the first fishermen had thrown the refuse of their catches out of doors. These cats were infinitely rapacious but discreet, having come to possess subtle powers of discrimination, by which they distinguished the forbidden from that which had been surrendered to them. The tail-less creature now eyeing the prize upon the slab controlled a servile following of younger cats who had learned to rely on its genius as a discoverer of food. Whenever it stopped, to test the atmosphere with sinister humility, they hesitated in the background. When, as now, with formal, elastic steps it moved nearer, they drew in. After a long, final deliberation, it sprang, to alight on the slab at the fish's side. And then the shadows all round gave up their eager, pouncing shapes.

CHAPTER 24

WHEN Costa awoke he was surprised to find himself in a half-forgotten childhood haunt; a place where in bygone years he had picnicked so often with the other children. There was the spring still dribbling from the rock and, below it, the dark, cobwebbed cistern into which he had thrown coins and wished for the good fortune which he was so confident would in any case be his. The little brick stoves all round, now partially overgrown, were still blackened with the fires which they had made there to cook their food so many years ago.

He got up and stretched himself to dislodge the cramps in his limbs, and then washed his hands and face in the cold spring water. The incidents of the past evening were coming back in an orderly and unhurried fashion, and Costa passed them in review as if they were the details of a pointless story that had happened to someone else. He felt mentally numbed, and the feeling was not unpleasant, because with it had come a sensation of freedom. This freedom had been won without effort. There had been no struggle to escape. He had merely walked out of an imprisoning room through a door which had always been open. He was mildly surprised that this escape should have been so long delayed. He noticed that he was deaf in one ear, but the pain had gone. He washed the blood out of his shirt in the spring, put it on wet, climbed down to the road, and set out to walk to the main Barcelona highway.

At the road junction Costa held up the first lorry that came along, walking out confidently, arm upraised, into the path of the oncoming vehicle. The driver, a small, tight-lipped man, looked surprised. He opened the door of the cabin and Costa climbed in. There was a silence which lasted through forty miles of farms and pinewoods; then the driver said: 'Going after a job, then?' 'No,' Costa said. 'I'm on my way to fetch someone back from Barcelona.' 'Ah,' said the driver. Half an hour later he said: 'Feel like a bite of something?' He handed Costa half a loaf and a piece of sobresada sausage. 'Go on, and take it all. I can't eat. Just lost my teeth. They were poisoning my system. Here, have something to wash it down.' He took one hand off the wheel to reach for a leathern bottle and the lorry swerved over the crown of the road. There was a fiercely hooted protest in the rear and, as they pulled in again, a big saloon car slipped past, then cut across so sharply that the lorry's front bumper scraped the rear wing of the car. The car's warning lights went on, and the driver, throwing all the weight of his small body on the brake pedal, pulled the lorry up with its radiator a foot from the suave corpulence of the car's rear. A big young man with a black moustache pencilled over his top lip, and a red spot in the middle of each cheek, bundled out and came at them arms waving. 'I've a good mind to knock the . . .' he started, then he saw Costa's face, and stopped.

'That's Barcelona for you,' said the driver, as they moved off again. 'Pigs, that's all. No manners.' Costa awoke to the fact that they were in the city's outskirts. He was unimpressed. Barcelona and its citizens had lost their power to intimidate. Only one thing remained unexplained. How was it that he had not seen this simple solution before? The thing was so straightforward. 'Girl I've been going with,' he explained to the driver. 'Working here as a domestic. Thought it was about time I took her away.'

The driver nodded his approval. 'Good thing, too. You don't want to let any decent girl hang around too long in a place like this. Where do you want me to drop you?'

The man in the fine uniform was nowhere to be seen, and there was an 'out of order' notice hanging on the gate of the service lift. Costa went up in the passenger lift with two strange, scented men. One of them was thin and elderly. His eyes were screwed up into an expression of pain borne with good humour, and although Costa's thoughts were elsewhere he could not take his eyes off the white gloves which the man wore, with their yellow net inserts. His companion was short and dark. He spoke with an Andalusian accent, and held himself with his chest thrown out like a cockerel. Neither man appeared aware of Costa's presence.

The white-gloved man was first out of the lift. He rang the doorbell, waited, and rang it again. He clicked his tongue impatiently, and stood aside shrugging his shoulders while the Andalusian pressed the bell-push twice. They heard the snap of the latch, electrically-released; the door opened a foot and a dehumanized, microphone voice invited them to make themselves comfortable in the waiting-room.

Costa found himself in a small white-walled chamber that reminded him of the new dentist's ante-room at Torre del Mar. They sat in tubular chromium-plated chairs. There was a glass-topped table with a small, strutted notice which said: 'Please do not offer cheques, as a refusal may offend.' Costa spelt through the words twice without understanding. The short man spoke in a whisper that filled every crevice of the bare room. 'I see they've changed things round again. Even electrified the maid.'

The other's expression of pain had become more acute. 'It's all so squalid, my dear friend. I can't bear it. The white paint gives me the jim-jams. They'll be tiling the walls next.'

'Personally I am not averse to cleanliness,' the Andalusian said. 'For me Barcelona still has nothing better to offer.' His words came in a deformed southern gabble.

'It's always the same,' the white-gloved man complained. 'You discover a place. It's a gem. You mention it to a friend or two, and the word gets round . . . Finished. Prices sky-high, and about as much character or charm left as a lavatory at an airport. They lose the personal touch.'

'If you permit me to speak frankly, I find you too difficult to please,' his friend said. 'Do you ever question yourself whether it is possible to lose something by being too fastidious?'

'I have never wished to wait in such a place at such a time of the morning. You, Pedro, are a man of singular pleasures.'

The short man craned his neck as if about to crow. 'I'm

a prey to my vitality at all hours of the day,' he said. They were both suddenly aware of Costa standing over them. 'Is this a whore-house?' Costa asked.

The two men stared at each other, eyebrows lifted, and the short man tittered.

'I'm afraid you'd be struck off the membership list if they heard you use a word like that for their temple of Venus,' the man with the white gloves said. 'They are — or used to be — most exclusive. Without wanting to be offensive, do you think you've come to the right address?'

'Where are they?' Costa asked.

'Where are who? — the resident faculty?'

'The people who work here. The whores.'

'On the other side of that door,' the white-gloved man said. 'We're far too soon, as usual. They'll unlock it when they're ready.' Seeing Costa go to the door, he said: 'They take their time. It's no use trying to hurry them.'

Costa went to the door and leaned on it and he heard the wood splinter as the lock gave way. He passed through slowly and uncertainly, into an ogre's palace full of gilt shapes, glass jewels and spying eyes. A garden of obscene lilies, mouthing at him, released a perfume of cigars. Fat-bodied cherubs leered from the ceiling and statues postured in the shadows. He passed from room to room under the glow of stifled lamps. Brushing through the silken cobwebs curtaining an alcove, he found a gross-bellied oriental god, squatting in the fumes of incense. He backed away, upsetting a dragon-carved table, and an overturned musical box began a silly tinkling. It was all as soft as the belly-fur of a Persian cat and as secret as a torture chamber. From this place the daylight had been sealed away for ever.

He was bewildered now, a bull trapped in a padded labyrinth, with the blood pounding in his temples, and his head full of the singing of the sea-shells pressed to his ears. A door opened as if in obedience to an idea and he was in a room with three girls, who were drinking coffee round a gramophone. He stared into their faces, a cup overturned and the needle jumped from the groove, cancelling a threadbare cadence of violins from 'Tales from the Vienna Woods'. A tall mirror swung at him and splintered and, in the clear space beyond a grey-haired woman like a wardress, a bunch of keys at her waist, was jabbing anxiously at the hook of the telephone.

Alarm bells jangled, someone blew a whistle again and again, and a small white dog that had been clipped into a woollen imitation of itself came at him leaping and snapping. A man, open-mouthed but silent, broke from a chrysalis of bed-clothes. Two girls swam from him, screeching, through the curling water of their night-dresses.

Costa crashed on, tearing away the tasselled cords that were looped for his throat and kicking aside the obstacles placed to trip him. Suddenly he was in a place where hard, white daylight pressed on his eyeballs, and a man in his shirt and trousers, with the braces hanging down, was tugging at the mechanism of an automatic pistol. Costa took the pistol and dropped it through the mouth that opened to receive it in the carpet's surface. As he did so he noticed the bed, and the form that slipped from it. It was no more than a glimpse that he got before the door slammed, but there was a trick of movement recalled, a streaming of familiar hair, a sound that might have been a wail cut short, that reminded him of the reason for his being there.

The man had torn the shade from a bedside lamp and, as Costa turned to him, he raised his arm and brought the lamp down on Costa's forehead. The room crackled with blue lightning. Costa heard the bulb explode, but felt nothing. He wiped the blood from his eyes. The man was standing with his back to the window, grinning with fear. Costa's attention was taken by a sound that had reached him from the street far below. It was the sound of a horn being blown. His memory lost its shape. There's a hunt on, he thought. Who are they hunting? Why, me, of course. No need to ask. I've always been hunted. Why must it be me? Why always me? What have I done?

Listening, he took a step forward, and the man struck at him again with the lamp. Costa brushed aside the blow. Suddenly he hated this man from the bottom of his soul. He was one of the hunters — the last of them, and the worst.

Never had the idea of hitting back until now, Costa said to himself. Always let them hunt me. Kept my head down, kept my mouth shut, kept away from them, hoped I'd get away in the end. But this was the end. He was cornered now, no way out, couldn't go any farther. The man's rat face came into focus again, teeth bared, and Costa remembered that there was one satisfaction, at least, he could take before they got him.

He picked the man up, and carried him to the open window.

CHAPTER 25

'AS you see, my cough's left me at last,' Don Federico said. 'I took myself in hand. As a result, I'm a new man.'

'How did you go about it?' Rosas asked. 'It might be of some importance to medical science to know.'

'Diet, that's all. I've been experimenting.'

'And what new fad have you embraced?'

'Fad? Oh come now, we all know it upsets you people to see a victim slip through your fingers. I decided that I was eating too much, so now I live on black beans and the view.' Vilanova threw out an arm in a gesture seawards.

'And does your housekeeper have to fit in with the new scheme of things?'

'Oh no, not at all. We go our separate ways. The view doesn't agree with her digestion, so she has something else to make up.'

'Well, don't cut out the beans, that's all I can say. You're practically transparent as it is.' Rosas shifted his position a little to allow a bunch of wisteria to shade the back of his neck from the sun's rays. 'What I really looked in for was to inquire after your son. Any further news?'

'No more than you've heard already. I expect he'll be back in a few days.'

'What are you going to do with him?'

'I'm going to tell him to take off his coat, roll up his sleeves, and get down to making something of this place,' Don Federico said.

Rosas surveyed the spare distinction of the land around them. This year a pest had stripped the leaves from the cork oaks, so that the green had gone out of the landscape which was silvered over with corroded metal. Sounds came to them clearly, unmuffled in foliage through the bare, writhing branches; the snapping of dogs in distant farmyards, an aerial tinkling of goats' bells, the bleat of a car horn in the bottom of the valley. The bare hilltops at the back of the landscape were the colour of mouldy chocolate. 'I can't see him doing much with this,' Rosas said.

'It's probably a blessing in disguise. There's a world glut of people in parasitic occupations.' Don Federico felt that it might assist in disguising his feelings if he used his binoculars. He directed them on the distant village square where, at that moment, freshly arrived tourists were soaking like a coloured stain from a bus into the whiteness of the houses. 'I can't understand what's been going on down there today,' he said. 'Nobody about the place, and the boats haven't gone out since this morning.'

'I was stopped by a guard on my way up,' Rosas said. 'Have you noticed they're half of them short-sighted? Part of the drive on smuggling, I suppose. Anyway, here comes your friend, the best informed man in Torre del Mar. I expect he'll be able to give us the facts.'

Don Federico looked down just as the beggar stopped, waving his stick. 'Ave Maria!' 'I do wish he wouldn't mumble so,' he said to nobody in particular. 'I still can't hear him half the time. Unless it's my faculties that are impaired.'

'Have you change for five pesetas?' he asked the beggar.

'I can't say I have.'

'Very well. I'll have the change next time.' He wedged the note in the cleft of the beggar's stick. 'What on earth's been going on down there today?'

'A man-hunt,' the beggar said. 'But without much excitement. By no means to compare with the ones they show us on the films.'

Rosas nodded in agreement. 'You must have sewers for a proper man-hunt. You can't imagine a really first-class hue and cry in this country. We're far too backward . . . Who are they after, smugglers?'

'No,' said the beggar, 'bandits. Or perhaps I should say a French bandit, the perpetrator of a number of atrocious murders. The village is full of policemen looking under beds. They're a stupider variety than usual. One of them actually went over me for concealed weapons on the way up here. By the way, I've brought a letter for you, Don Federico. The postmistress was too nervous to come out.' The beggar stuck the letter in the end of the cleft stick and reached it up.

'The bandit,' Rosas said, '— how did they come to track him down to this place?'

'They didn't. Of all people to choose to lodge with, he picked on Costa. Needless to say, Costa gave him away.'

Vilanova had opened his letter. He put it down. 'Why needless to say?'

'Because everyone knew he was hand in glove with the police.'

'No, they didn't,' Vilanova said. 'Nothing of the kind. I didn't, for one.'

'If the man murdered a Frenchman, it's the business of the French to look after him,' said the beggar. 'As I see it, that doesn't justify Costa turning him in. Still, what can you expect in these times when cuckolds carry the banners in the sacred processions . . . Anything much in that letter?'

'I can't read it,' Vilanova said. 'And may I say I don't like your attitude? You jump to conclusions.' He held up the typewritten sheet and scrutinized it again, eyes narrowed. 'In conformity with the powers conferred under disposition . . . you are hereby informed that the areas scheduled in the accompanying . . .' He passed the paper over to Rosas: 'Here you read this, and tell me what it says. It's one of these official things. Always takes me half an hour trying to find out what on earth they're talking about.'

Rosas took the paper and read it. He re-read it, frowning, turned it over and looked at the back, examined the date-stamp on the envelope, put it down.

'What's it all about?' Don Federico asked. 'More taxes?'

Rosas's lips were pursed. He took a breath. 'They want your land.'

'Who wants it?' Don Federico asked mildly.

'Some department or other. Ministry of War, I believe.' He picked up the paper and went over a passage. 'It's not clear from this whether they're prepared to let you live on in the house, but they're going to turn the area into some sort of firing-range, so it's on your own head if you get hurt.'

'I won't give it up,' Vilanova said, his voice unchanged. 'I wouldn't even dream of it.'

'Not voluntarily, no, of course you won't. But I'm afraid they'll have it all the same. What'll probably happen is that you'll get some sort of an official notification of the day they're taking over, which you'll tear up without reading; then one day in a few months' time, when you're beginning to hope they've forgotten all about you, they'll turn up with the notices and the barbed wire, and that will be that. Naturally there'll be some sort of compensation.'

Don Federico was blinking as if he was looking into strong sunlight. There was a silence, and then, as if explaining some new circumstance to Rosas, he said: 'They want to take it away from me.'

'Yes,' Rosas said.

Don Federico's eye went quickly and anxiously round the barren beauty of his acres. 'It's not fair, is it?' he said.

There was another long silence. The beggar's parting salutation went unanswered, and Rosas heard him shuffle off down the road. He leaned forward and squeezed the old man's arm affectionately.

'I don't know what to do,' Don Federico said.

Rosas tried to think of something to say that would refute the chilling finality of those typewritten sentences. An idea came to him. 'Perhaps it's not so hopeless as it seems. I believe I know of someone who might be able to help. We'd have to move quickly.'

Don Federico said: 'I want to die here. Really, there's nothing more I ask from life. Just to be left in peace. I'm too old to pull up my roots now.'

'I know a man called Valls,' Rosas said. 'I wouldn't like to be too optimistic, but if there's anyone who could do anything in a case like this . . .'

'No,' said Vilanova.

'You know of him?'

'Yes,' said Vilanova, 'I know of him.'

'He's our only hope,' Rosas said. 'I admit I understand your prejudice.'

Indignation had steadied Don Federico's nerves and cleared his wits. 'I happen to know what Valls's terms would be for any assistance he felt like giving. I'd just as soon see my land hacked to bits by the War department as let Valls get his paws on it.' He looked at Rosas suspiciously. 'That monster hasn't been getting at you, I hope?'

'You're an old fool,' Rosas said. 'Sometimes I wonder why I bother with you. As it is, I'm the only friend you've got.'

'Yes,' said Vilanova. 'That's perfectly true, too.'

Maria had come up and taken a seat facing them across the table. 'Well,' she said, 'so you're finally in the soup this time. And now what do you propose to do?'

Vilanova looked at her affectionately. She was one of those fine, rare women who only felt able to display the quality of their love when things went wrong. A beautiful woman, too, in her time, who hadn't had one tenth of her deserts from life. 'I'm a failure, my dear,' he said. 'Unfortunately it is not only myself I let down.'

'For God's sake don't snivel like that,' she said. 'You're at your worst when you snivel.'

'I see no reason why you should share in my dejection,' Vilanova said. 'You've always detested this place.'

'Of course I've detested it. What woman wouldn't? It's as bad as a prison. But if you want to live in misery, I suppose it's good enough for me.' She turned away quickly to dab at an eye. 'I came to tell you that the foxes got two more of your beloved chickens this morning.'

'The cannibals!' he shouted, mechanically wrathful, but the fire in him died away immediately. 'Two of them?' he said in a bewildered voice.

'Including your prize cockerel — the one with the bandy legs. I've put what's left of the carcase in the tool shed for you to bait the trap with.'

Vilanova sat there, eyes unfocused, hearing Maria's voice but incapable for the moment of extracting the meaning from the words. 'The foxes,' he said. 'Of course — the foxes.'

'Yes,' she said, 'the foxes. At the rate they're going, they'll have cleaned up what's left of the poultry in a week. What I'd like to know is if you propose to do anything about it, or whether you expect me to do your work as well as my own?'

'I must do something about it,' Don Federico said.

'Well, do it now,' she said. 'If you'd have done as I told you before, this wouldn't have happened. Anybody'll tell you the place to set the trap is by their holes, not in the chicken house. Why should they want to bother about dead meat when they can get all the live chickens they want?'

'Am I expected to do this now?'

'Why not? If you put it off you'll forget again.' She

exchanged a quick glance with the doctor. 'I'll look after Doctor Rosas.'

Don Federico got up. 'You're nagging me,' he said.

'In case I don't see you when you get back, Don Federico . . .' Rosas began.

Vilanova turned back. 'Oh, of course. You're still there.' He remembered something. 'And by the way, Rosas, there's to be no plotting behind my back about Valls. Absolutely nothing doing, you know, in that direction.'

CHAPTER 26

DON FEDERICO went to the outhouse, found the gory remnants of the cockerel where Maria had left it, and dropped it into a sack. The fox-holes were some distance from the house in the decayed sandstone of a ruined cliff through which the sea had broken to form a narrow bay.

He set out along the narrow path cut through brambles and the fragrant bitter weeds that every year moved up their frontiers closer to the house, picking his way perhaps a hundred paces, then stopped. Below him a skin of water glistened through the stencilled leaves. His eye was taken by an aerial movement where two of his tumbler pigeons, rising and falling as if linked together, burnished a patch of sky with their wings. Don Federico had the sensation that he was waiting for something to happen and, as he watched, interest half engaged, a falcon curved out of space, rigid-winged, and one of the pigeons had vanished, leaving a single feather to come twisting earthwards. Incredible, he thought. The blight in the oaks, the foxes and the falcon. It was as if the malevolent intuition of the natural world had marked his downfall, and the devourers of defenceless flesh would wait no longer for their prey. He threw the sack he was carrying into a bush. If they were in a hurry to divide the spoils, what did it matter? let them come!

This, thought Don Federico, is the fashion in which a

family arrives at the end of the road; the meaningless, dusty details of dissolution. Well, so be it. If we've gone down, it's because we've deserved no better. We've always thought of ourselves as aristocrats, but really we've been as unenterprising as peasants who manage to live through the whole of history in one spot and leave nothing behind them but a hundred-foot-high mound of broken water-pots, lost coins, dogs' bones and the dry dust of concealed births pushed away under the floors. From now on we'll be peasants in name as well, people who only live to exist. My son will be the peasant, and Valls's son will try his hand at being the aristocrat. Good luck to him.

There's only been one of us in the whole of our history as a family, he thought, that left any mark, and he remembered again the ancestor who on a day in spring in the year 1560 had met his end in the field outside the walls of Seville — used, as the occasion demanded, for horse fairs or the burning of heretics. There was little known of this man beyond the facts relating to his death, which had been the result of the slightest possible difference between an official viewpoint and the one he had held personally, and had not felt able to concede. The elegance of bearing of Vilanova's ancestor on this sombre and spectacular occasion had passed into legend. And so this silent and smiling man had taken his leave of the world's mediocrity, quietly moving up to occupy his place at the head of the family for all time. Those who followed him had been sadly overshadowed, carrying on in a bloodless way their tradition of guarded disapproval, non-belligerence and sitting-on-the-fence, in which he had been a champion.

In the bitter illumination of this moment Vilanova saw that his own revolt against an order of things which he detested had been indistinguishable from the grumblings of a crotchety old man. It had come to be regarded as a mere eccentricity; to such as Rosas, even a lovable one.

Don Federico's feet carried him forward, picking their way independently of his conscious direction over the roughness of a path they had followed a thousand times. Then he found he was no longer walking and, coming back to earth, realized that he had reached the large, comfortably-shaped boulder on which he usually rested when taking this walk. With the mildest sensation of surprise Don Federico noticed that this time his place was already occupied. At his approach, the man who had been lying prone on the flat-topped rock hoisted himself into a sitting position. Vilanova saw a small grey-yellow face, with the flesh gone back like a tide from the cheek-bones, with blood on the eye-lashes and at the parting of the lips. It occurred to him as an afterthought that it was surprising that the man's clothes were wet and clinging to the protuberances of his bony frame. Water bubbled in the seams of his shoes as he made an effort to stand, and the spongy surface of the stone was soaking up a long, wet patch where he had lain.

This man's expression held the same stunned, stubborn disbelief as Vilanova had once seen in the face of a condemned man being hustled away to the garrotting post.

The extremity of the moment had induced in Don Federico's brain a kind of drugged passivity. He was living through an apocalyptic minute when it was natural that the lion should lie down with the lamb. 'Je suppose,' he said calmly, 'que vous êtes le bandit?'

For the half-drowned Molina, too, intuition was in control of an enfeebled reason, and Don Federico seemed a being from another world, cleansed of earthly partisanship.

'I'm a political fugitive,' he said in Spanish. 'The police are after me.' He stood up and rivulets of sea water tinged with blood ran down the backs of his hands.

'Are you hurt?' Don Federico said.

'I took poison and fell into the water. The poison didn't work.'

'I suppose you've given it sufficient time?' Don Federico asked, with a kind of automatic solicitude.

Molina measured the slackening of the waves of his nausea and shook his head. 'It's immediate or not at all. Must have vomited it back in the water.' He belched and his mouth filled with salt liquid. Shuddered, then recovering, he said with grotesque formality: 'I'm obliged to take my life immediately.' The poison and the sea water combined had left him as drunk as if he had swallowed half a bottle of brandy.

'Why immediately?' Don Federico asked.

'Because I can't get away. They're all round. Men and dogs. No hope.'

'Have you ever considered that they can't do more than kill you? Even if it comes to the worst, they'll make a cleaner job of it than you seem capable of doing.'

Molina raised himself again, swaying, and said with a sudden fierceness: 'Too many other lives involved. If they once get their hands on me it's all up with them, too.'

'I see,' Vilanova said. 'You mean you realize that you can't stand pain.'

'It's no use,' Molina said. 'It doesn't matter whether you can stand it or you can't. They're scientific these days. You're a lunatic as far as they are concerned. So you get treatment — electric shocks, at the most a small brain operation. Hundred per cent results. Why even bother about old-fashioned tortures?'

'That being so, I must agree that you've no alternative.'

As Don Federico spoke, they both heard the distant, brief escape of sound, immediately checked, of a dog barking, and then from a different direction immediately below them, as the sea paused, a snatch of voices, clear and close. Molina shivered and turned away.

'Can you walk?' Don Federico asked. He took Molina by the arm. 'I think we must conclude that that's a boat arriving.' Attempting to steady Molina, he found himself staggering as they moved off, side by side, up the path.

'In a way I'm in a similar predicament to your own,' Don Federico said, 'although in my case the issues can't be said to be so urgent. It's really most unfortunate for the pair of us that we're living in the present century. My house was designed to deal with this kind of situation. A few generations back it would have been so simple — just a matter of going in, closing the front door, and waiting for our pursuers to go home . . . I hope you aren't feeling faint?'

'It's passing,' Molina said. 'A few more minutes and I'll be myself again.'

'In that case, perhaps we should accelerate our pace,'

Vilanova said. 'Even if I felt prepared to accept the indignity of running the last fifty metres, I'm not sure I could manage it.'

They turned a corner of the path and were confronted by the first of the decayed farm buildings, with their two small yellow volcanoes of haystacks surmounted by chamberpots, the meagre results of a share-cropping tenant's harvest. Immediately behind arose the sheer, curving wall of the house, moulded from the weather-beaten outcrop of rock on which it stood, with cement spread like a confection between the massive, shapeless stones, and the white-rimmed, sleepless eye of a single tiny window peering out at thirty feet from the ground.

Don Federico paused for a moment to regain breath. 'The last siege,' he said, in a mildly pedagogic tone, 'was undertaken by a bishop over some question of the withholding of ecclesiastical dues. A cannon which was brought by sea fell into the water while they were unloading it. I'm told it's still there. In those days it used to be the Church and the foreigners. It's only in recent times that the State's turned into the principal menace.' They moved forward again, Don Federico holding Molina's arm. 'Only a few more yards. I think we've timed it rather well.'

They went in through the enormous double gates, only one side of which was half open. Don Federico said: 'I'm afraid I shall have to trouble you to help me close this. My father had a positive mania for security. Not satisfied with six inches of oak, he actually went to the trouble of lining these gates with metal. As a result, no one of normal physique can move the things on their hinges.' There was a quick slap of footsteps over a stone floor above them, and they saw Maria, black-draped, pass behind the headless stone lions that decorated the gallery, and then come down the open staircase at the back of the courtyard. Don Federico called to her: 'Do help us put up these bars, my dear. I can't help feeling that some very simple mechanical device could have been made to do all this kind of thing.'

Maria arrived at the bottom of the staircase, taking in Molina's condition with a quick scrutiny. 'What have you been up to now?' she asked Don Federico.

'We've a bottle of exceptional brandy somewhere in the house, have we not?' Vilanova asked. 'This is an old friend of mine. As you see, he's very wet and rather the worse for wear. We're going to celebrate something.'

'And what, if one might ask?' she said, looking at Molina with the hostility of a woman whose husband has ruined some occasion of sentimental solemnity by arriving home with an obvious ne-er-do-well.

'The day of the fox.'

'The day of the what did you say?'

'The fox,' he said. 'All the foxes of various kinds. Did Rosas go home? God bless him.'

'You're acting very strangely,' she said.

'I've a right to. I'm in a state of nervous exaltation. After all they're going to take my place away.' He turned to Molina. 'You may have noticed the tower at the side of the house. Forty years ago I'd have been quite capable of taking a gun up to the top of it and picking a few of them off as they came. Just as well I'm an old man, because I used to be a good shot, and I'd have killed the wrong people. The ones you can get at with a gun are always the wrong ones.'

Molina said: 'But it's me they're after, not you.'

'Of course they are,' Don Federico said. 'And I want to do something for you. That's why we've come here. What can I do? That's the question.'

'I only need a weapon,' Molina said with forced resolution. At that moment they heard a scuffle of footsteps outside the gate. Don Federico made a grimace and, signing to Molina, he led the way across the courtyard through an open door into a cell-like room containing a rough table, a few chairs and a picture of the Crucifixion. Maria came in carrying the brandy and two glasses. She put them down on the table and stood there watching Molina, indignation quivering in the muscles of her face. 'Go and get another glass,' Don Federico told her. 'I want you to drink with us. It's a special occasion.' To Molina he said, 'You were talking about a weapon. I'm to take it that you're still determined to do away with yourself?'

Molina nodded. 'Absolutely.'

'I won't attempt to deter you. It would be dishonourable to do so.' He raised his glass. 'Long live whatever you've been fighting for, and may our enemies lack good brandy to warm the straw in their guts when it comes to their turn!' Vilanova drained his glass, got up and went out of the room and came back carrying a coil of rope. He threw the rope down on the table. 'Here you are. Here's your weapon.'

Molina took the rope and uncoiled it. Through the doorway they could hear that the noise outside the gate had increased, and now there was a knocking. Molina felt the harsh edges of the strands. Watching his face closely, Don Federico said: 'Silk strangles just as well as hemp.' He nodded towards an opening at the far end of the room. 'There's a hook in the pantry ceiling.'

Molina got up, taking the rope, then stopped. He passed a hand over his face, wiping away a dew of sweat that had suddenly appeared. 'Have you a gun?' he asked.

Don Federico said: 'Unfortunately I can offer you the choice of only two weapons; the one you hold in your hand, and a fall of some sixty feet from the top of our tower on to its foundation of solid rock. I'm sorry for you, because I now see you lack a real aptitude for despair. Without the blessing of true despair these things are hard to face.' There was a heavy banging on the gate and a voice shouted incoherently through the narrow separation of the wood. Don Federico reached for the bottle again. 'In the old days they could have banged away for half a week. Even now we've got a couple of hours to fill in before someone thinks of sending for dynamite.'

'A couple of hours?'

'If we decide there's any point in keeping them waiting as long as that. However, I've a proposal to make in case you're still interested in a somewhat remote possibility of getting away.'

Molina's pulse quickened as if in response to a transfusion of fresh blood. He would have clutched at the slightest hope of reprieve as a martyr might have embraced the certainty of heaven. In his extremity he had become shameless. 'I'm a coward,' he said to Don Federico. 'I forced myself to accept death once today. It's broken me.

There's nothing left. It's a thousand times worse now.'

'And quite understandably,' Don Federico said. 'If you really decide to die, then you've a right to die and get it over. You had bad luck with that poison.'

Molina's self-disgust was choking him. 'I'm actually relieved to be alive.'

'That proves you're a sick man. You're in no decent condition to die. If you had a few hours to pull yourself together you'd probably feel perfectly up to the mark again. Hence my suggestion. I can't see that there's the slightest chance of your getting right away, but it might at least give you a breathing space.'

Maria came into the room. 'The garden's full of police,' she said. 'They've got a ladder.'

'Confound them!' Don Federico said. 'I can imagine the mess the brutes are making among the flowers. It's not as if they've the faintest hope of breaking in that way. The back door's like the entrance to a bank vault. Allow me to refill your glass. I'm loath to leave any of this excellent brandy to be finished off by people who might not appreciate it.'

Molina emptied his glass and Don Federico refilled it. He poured out a third glass and put it in Maria's hand. 'Darling, I'm sorry we couldn't have had a long talk about things. There's a letter for you in the box under my bed. I've mislaid the key. You'll have to break it open.'

'Don't be melodramatic,' she said. She tightened her lips.

'I should make a trip into Barcelona and fix up with any dealer in the Calle de Paja for the furniture. There's nothing to choose among them in point of dishonesty.

Don't let Valls get his paws on anything . . . and my apologies for the melodrama. It's the fable of the wolf over again. Well,' he said to Molina, 'it's time you thought of your departure.'

He got up and led the way through the dark, resounding emptiness of the house through sallow chambers strangely shaped by the needs of other days, and out into a second courtyard that was almost filled by the watch-tower's massive base.

'If only we could see the past again,' Don Federico said. 'How often must the people of this house have taken refuge here from the human beasts of their day!' He pushed open a door in the tower with his foot and out of the darkness an odour came to them of the silent, abandoned decay of forgotten centuries.

'You are favoured by the fact that miserable rates of pay attract only people of inferior mentality into the police,' Don Federico said. 'There's an emergency exit from this tower, a subterranean passage a few hundred yards in length that comes out on the hillside over there, overlooking the sea. Nothing extraordinary about it. All these places employed the same system. The tunnel's entrance at the other end used to be hidden, but now children play in it. It's so familiar that everyone's forgotten its existence. There's a cove just below and the remnants of a boat-house with my boat in it. Whether the boat's still sound or not, I can't tell you. It's a year or two since I last entrusted myself to the water. For all I know it may sink like a stone, but whatever its condition it's yours for the taking.'

Molina groped his way forward. 'You'll see the trap

door when your eyes get used to the darkness. The bolt works quite easily. As soon as you're ready I'll lock the door behind you and throw the key down the well.'

Don Federico brought his hand from behind his back and held it out and Molina found himself holding a huge old-fashioned pistol.

'It's ancient,' Vilanova said, 'but dreadfully effective. If it comes to the worst, the roof of the mouth's the place. I've known a man to survive a shot in the temple.'

He went away murmuring to himself: 'Most unsalubrious. Wild horses couldn't have dragged me down that horrible hole in the ground.'

'You know,' Don Federico said to Maria, a few moments later, 'people should be able to die as they do on the films, without undignified preliminaries, delays, and obvious mutilations . . . And now, if you'll excuse me, I'll go and titivate a little before admitting our friends out there. I feel that this is a rather important occasion and I should like to be able to feel that I was looking my best.'

CHAPTER 27

'WELL,' said the colonel, 'I'd hardly call this particular operation a success.'

'No, sir.'

'It's unbelievable that the man could have been allowed to slip through our fingers in the way he was. I'm not putting the blame on you personally. It was badly handled from above. Too many fingers in the pie.'

'Yes, sir,' Calles said.

'For God's sake, sit down. Really I don't know what the service is coming to. I'm not exaggerating when I say that when I started my career it couldn't have happened even if they'd given us the Sierra Nevada itself to find our man in.' The fraud of memory foisted on the colonel an heroic picture of himself in the days before he had worn promotion and success like a fatty tissue, flying rather than riding his charger through the bleached bone of the high sierras. He blew out a little air sadly. On the previous day he had decided that the time had come to finish his poem; now he was suffering from the flatness and anti-climax of achievement. An essential rhythm had been suppressed, and his mind felt untidy and at a loose end.

The colonel went to the window and was a little soothed by the view of Torre del Mar which, in the evening light, had gone as sentimental as a painting of it by a foreign visitor. Below him the patio was filled with lemon trees with the lemons hanging carved into new moons by the dark leaves. 'You realize,' he said, coming back, 'that old Vilanova's making a laughing stock of us?'

'I was given to understand he was proving co-operative, sir.'

'Co-operative? What a word! So far he's filled fifty typewritten sheets with depositions. We can't persuade him to stop talking. At first we were tempted to give some credence to his stories, and then he actually had the audacity to claim complicity in the Fossa power-station outrage. That means we're put to the trouble of re-opening the case. I ask you, lieutenant, can you see that old fellow as one of the key men in any organization? The old villain. You should see the look in his eye. He's out to give us all the trouble he can . . . By the way, has anything further come to light about Molina?'

'An individual called Gomez, alias Cabrera, the proprietor of a beach refreshment hut, was found in possession of several planks from the missing boat. He made a statement to the effect that he had found the boat smashed up in the rocks.' Calles remembered something. 'There have been several instances of bodies washed ashore at this spot, sir. It's supposed to be something to do with the currents.'

'But no body this time?'

'Gomez denies finding one, although his clothes were all beachcomber's salvage.'

'And is he to be relied upon?'

'No sir, he's an intellectual.'

'A what?'

'An intellectual. A man with the worst possible record. The first thing we found when we investigated his background was that he deserted from the Nationalists and went over to the Reds. They promoted him to the command of one of the Militias of Culture.'

The colonel shuddered.

'Since then he has succeeded in covering his tracks by faking loss of memory. We soon cured him of that.'

'Was he helpful?'

'I've no hesitation in saying that he was the worst and most stubborn case in my experience of the service.'

'Just the man in fact that might have been expected to help Molina get away.'

'If he could have, sir. There's no doubt about that. On the other hand they say here that no ordinary swimmer could have got very far in that sea.'

And that, thought the colonel, is about as much as we'll ever know about this particular mystery. We tugged at the weed, he thought, and it broke away in our hands, leaving the roots to go on growing. Old Vilanova who looked upon prison as a joke was in gaol, while his son, harbouring a bitter grievance, had managed to get out of the country, and would be preparing his share of trouble for the years to come. 'Would you care to hear the situation report, sir?' the lieutenant's voice broke in, and the colonel, his mind far away, nodded his assent.

Calles began to record in his toneless, official voice the trivial oppressions, the restrictions of movement, the fines for illegal possession, the continuing surveillance of notorious ex-Reds. Obliged in the end to listen, the colonel found himself irritated beyond measure. You, my friend, he wanted to say, are the product of a short-lived epoch in our national history that's already passing. Get that into your head. You're out of date. What's needed now, even in the police, is men with the genius to interpret Spanish laws in a Spanish fashion. The days of the mad dogs are over. Let's hear no more about Reds, or Falangists either. Haven't we as a people the greatness of heart to admit it's possible we were both wrong? His nose wrinkled. 'What on earth's that smell? It's burning up the membranes of my nose.'

Calles looked surprised. 'I believe it may be the Zotal I have the room washed out with, sir. The village smells so badly of fish.'

The colonel took out his handkerchief and sniffed the eau-de-Cologne. On the spur of the moment he took a decision. 'It may come as a surprise to you to hear that you're to be transferred shortly.'

The lieutenant gulped, his eyes correctly fixed on a point in space a few inches over the colonel's head.

'Well, *are* you surprised?'

'Yes, sir.'

'But not particularly sorry?'

'No, sir.'

'In case you should think this decision has anything to do with the recent unfortunate business, let me assure you it hasn't. The fact is the service can't afford to have you carrying out your duties among people you despise. It makes for inefficiency.'

'I quite understand, sir.'

He's being badly treated, the colonel thought, made a scapegoat, but it can't be helped. 'Have you any special preferences regarding a posting?' he asked.

'None, sir.'

'And nothing to say, either, I gather.'

Calles braced himself for an effort. 'Yes, sir. I should like to ask a favour.'

'A favour, lieutenant?' The colonel was slightly relieved. 'Well, if there's anything I can do . . .'

'I beg your pardon, sir, I wish to apply . . . that is to say there's an unfortunate case that's occurred here and I was wondering whether in the circumstances something couldn't be done on a higher level?'

'Go on,' the colonel said.

'An individual by the name of Costa's involved.'

'The name's very familiar.'

'You supplied a recommendation, sir. Perhaps you'll recollect he was a hero of the Movement. Molina happened to be lodging with his mother.'

'Of course. You found him a useful man, didn't you?'

'Most useful and co-operative, sir. Unfortunately he's got himself into serious trouble.'

'How serious?'

'A charge of murder, sir.'

'Murder! I don't recollect any mention of it in your report?'

'The crime was committed in Barcelona. It appears that his fiancée unwittingly took up domestic employment in a house of prostitution and was seduced by the owner. It's a recognized method they use for recruiting girls.'

'Well?'

'Costa got to hear about this.'

'And then?'

'He was involved in a dispute with the man.'

'A dispute you call it! Didn't you say he finished him off?'

'The attack seems to have been the result of a brainstorm. I've seen a copy of the medical report. There was clearly no premeditation, sir.'

'And why should you assume that?'

'Because no weapon was used.'

'Then what was the cause of death?'

'In the course of the altercation the victim was precipitated from a fifth floor window.'

'Defenestration,' said the colonel. 'Interesting. A classical touch about that. And what, may I ask, is your object in bringing those facts to my notice?'

'There might be grounds for reducing the charge to manslaughter, sir, if the matter were taken up at the proper level.'

'Might there? Nice of you to tell me. Am I to suppose you're actually asking me to use my influence at the proper level, as you put it?'

'I regard Costa as a comrade-in-arms, sir,' the lieutenant said.

'So you *are* asking me! Well, I suppose there's something to be said for being perfectly frank about those things.' For the first time since the colonel had known Calles he approved of him. 'Where's the girl in the case?' he asked.

'She's back in the village, sir.'

'Is she well?'

'I believe so, sir.'

'No ill effects? Health unimpaired? Not pregnant by any chance?'

'I've been given to understand that a difficulty of some such kind arose, but it's been taken care of by public subscription. I've not inquired into the details.'

'Have you ever studied the customary laws of the ancient kingdom of Aragon, lieutenant?' the colonel asked, with a sudden change of tone.

'No, sir.'

'You should do so. They're humane, broad-minded, and full of common sense. I only mention them because a condemned man on the scaffold was often offered a reprieve if he would agree to take a fallen woman as his wife. Does the idea surprise you, lieutenant?'

'I must admit it does, sir.'

'You'd be more surprised still if you knew how many turned the offer down.'

Calles did his best to look astonished. He saw the direction the conversation was taking.

'Now this man Costa, lieutenant. Just imagine, for example, that we let him off lightly. Does he strike you as the kind of man who might be expected to take the girl back?'

'I don't know, sir.'

'Then find out, lieutenant, find out. Why the devil should either of us expect the law to be more enlightened than the people it's designed to protect?'